"YOU'RE COVERED, DON'T MOVE."

Sip Ambrose halted dead in his tracks. Mayberly stepped close and snatched the revolver from Sip's gunbelt. Then he took a step sideways and turned cautiously. He found himself looking into the muzzle of a rifle held by Yadkin.

"Drop the gun," Yadkin said. "We'll take over now."

"You can go to hell," Mayberly said. "He's my prisoner."

Yadkin swung the barrel of his rifle against the side of Mayberly's head. A second blow came straight down on his skull and felled him...

Berkley Books by William O. Turner

A MAN CALLED JEFF
BLOOD DANCE
MAYBERLY'S KILL

WILLIAM O. TURNER

MAYBERLY'S KILL

BERKLEY BOOKS, NEW YORK

This Berkley book contains the complete
text of the original hardcover edition.
It has been completely reset in a type face
designed for easy reading, and was printed
from new film.

MAYBERLY'S KILL

A Berkley Book / published by arrangement with
Doubleday & Company

PRINTING HISTORY
Doubleday & Company edition published 1969
Berkley edition / July 1977
Third printing / March 1982

ISBN: 0-425-05479-9

A BERKLEY BOOK ® TM 757,375
Berkley Books are published by Berkley Publishing Corporation,
200 Madison Avenue, New York, New York 10016.
PRINTED IN THE UNITED STATES OF AMERICA

1

ZACK MAYBERLY sat with the scrubbed surface of the kitchen table between him and the girl. She was small and slender with a delicate face and black eyes. She was young. Nineteen, she said. She sat very straight and looked him in the eye and answered his questions readily. A little too readily, he thought.

"How long did you live up there on Grizzly Creek?"

"Since I married Eduardo. That was in February, two years ago."

"And Eduardo was killed Wednesday, the fourth of April? Three weeks ago tomorrow?"

"Yes."

The room was dark, low-ceilinged, a typical Mexican kitchen. Susanna Velasquez was not Mexican. This was the house of her sister-in-law, Eduardo's sister. Mayberly sat with his back to an open door that led to the parlor. Susanna sometimes looked past him and he was aware that the sister-in-law was in there, probably watching and listening. That was unimportant, but it made him nervous to sit with his back to a doorway. He got up and moved to a chair at the end of the table. This brought him closer to Susanna, who eyed him curiously.

"Your husband was killed by a horse?"

"He was kicked in the head. I found him in the barn—dead. I came into town for the doctor anyway. He and the deputy went back with me.''

Mayberly had spoken with the doctor and with the deputy. The doctor said Eduardo had died of a skull fracture. Far as he could tell, it could have been caused by a kick from a horse. The deputy said there was no reason to believe otherwise.

''You were living there alone with him at the time?''

''Yes.''

''What about the two men who had been staying with you?''

''They had left.''

''How long before Eduardo was killed?''

''Several days. Let's see. They left on a Friday. He was killed the next Wednesday.''

''They had lived with you for two years?''

''Not that long. Over a year, though. They weren't there all the time. They were prospectors and made our place their headquarters. They paid us board. They were gone most of the time in the summers, camping out. In the winter, they lived with us. Sometimes they went out when there was a thaw.''

''What were their names?''

''Mr. Lang and Mr. Dyer.''

''You always called them 'Mister'?''

''Yes.''

''What did your husband call them?''

''Sometimes he left off the 'Mister.' Their first names were Al and George. Is that what you're getting at?''

''Is that what they called each other—Al and George?''

''Yes.''

''Never anything else?''

''If you mean did I ever hear anything to suggest that their real names were something other than Al Lang and

2

George Dyer, the answer is no."

"It never occurred to you that they might be brothers?"

"Brothers? That's ridiculous. Mr. Lang is a big man. He's as tall as you are and heavier. Mr. Dyer is a skinny little thing. Their eyes are different too."

She had got herself into a small trap and a catching of her breath revealed that she knew it. He pressed his advantage gently.

"What color were Lang's eyes?"

"I'm not sure. I just remember that they were different."

"They were blue, weren't they? Pale blue?"

"Maybe they were. I wouldn't swear to it."

"That would make Dyer's eyes dark. Is that right?"

She laughed, shifting her position in her chair. "Have it your way, Mr. Mayberly. But I'm not sure about the eyes. And I certainly don't believe they were brothers. Why would they lie? I don't see what you're getting at."

"You've heard of the Ambrose brothers?"

"Ambrose? The outlaws?"

"One is big and solid. The other is a runt."

She looked at him squarely, eyebrows raised, eyes wide. That, alone, might have indicated honest surprise. But her next reaction followed too quickly and was altogether too positive. If she were truly startled, she would have had a moment of uncertainty, he thought.

"You've got yourself a wild-goose chase for sure," she said, laughing. "Those two were prospectors and harmless as lambs."

He was tempted to ask her about the beatings that the doctor had treated her for, but he thought better of it. Let her lie, he thought. Let her think you believe her. You'll learn more that way. Shake her confidence in herself as a liar and she'll tighten up to yes and no.

"They do a lot of heavy drinking?" he asked.

"No, sir. Oh, they had whisky around. On Christmas Eve we made toddies and we were all singing carols. It was awful! But heavy drinking—no."

Eduardo Velasquez had come in for supplies once a month or a little oftener, according to the local storekeeper. He had usually taken a case of whisky back with him and in at least one instance he had taken back two. And Mayberly had been out to the cabin on Grizzly Creek. He had found empty bottles and fragments of bottles everywhere. In the cabin, the barn, the woods behind the barn, the creek.

"And now the most important question. Where did Lang and Dyer say they were going when they left?"

"I'm sorry to disappoint you. They didn't."

"You didn't ask?"

"I suppose I might have. I don't think they knew, themselves."

"They didn't talk about their plans in front of you?"

"No—if they had any. They did mention Denver once in a while. They liked Denver. I wouldn't be surprised if they went back there."

Well done, he thought. She had planted a clue, a false clue, without seeming too positive or too eager. Wherever the two men had headed for, the chances were good it wasn't Denver.

The sister-in-law came into the kitchen, a big dark woman in her thirties. She went to the fireplace at the end of the room and poked at the coals. It was a way of saying he had stayed long enough.

"What will you do now?" he asked Susanna.

"I've got some relatives up north. Perhaps I'll go

4

there.''

''She is welcome to stay here,'' the sister-in-law said, speaking with the lilt and precision of a person used to Spanish. ''But in this house she must behave herself, so she will go away and get into trouble.''

Susanna made a face at her. ''Don't count on it. You may be stuck with me.''

Mayberly got to his feet. ''A girl as pretty as you are will have a lot of suitors. Take your time and pick a rich one.''

Susanna laughed, but the sister-in-law was offended. ''She will look a long time before she finds another man as good as my brother,'' she said.

Susanna gave him a secret wink. It was clear enough that she was not grieving for Eduardo, she was making no pretense. At lease she was being honest about that.

''Thank you for your patience,'' Mayberly said.

He turned into the living room toward the front door, the way he had come in. The sister-in-law followed him.

''You came with a note from the deputy sheriff,'' she said. ''We are glad to have a deputy here in Dos Pinos and we wish to be courteous.''

''You've been very courteous. I'll say as much to the deputy.''

When he had gone, she went back to the kitchen. Susanna was still at the table. ''A fool,'' she said. ''A bounty hunter chasing wild geese.''

''What is this about the Ambrose brothers? Is it possible?''

''Nonsense,'' Susanna said. ''They were two harmless prospectors.''

''Then why did you lie? Why did you say they were gone five days before Eduardo was killed? I know they were not. Eduardo was in town the day before he died. He came to visit for a few minutes. He said the prospectors were leaving in a day or two!''

Susanna sighed heavily. "It's simple enough. Mr. Lang and Mr. Dyer were afraid there would be an investigation and they wouldn't be able to leave. So I lied and said they had already left."

"*Ay de Dios* To lie to a bounty hunter is perhaps not a serious thing, but you have also lied to the deputy. And to me. Have I not the right to know the truth of my brother's death?"

"You know it," Susanna said gently. "I found Eduardo in the barn just as I told it."

"But if these prospectors are possibly the Ambrose brothers, could not one of them—"

"The Ambrose brothers! Felicia, this bounty hunter has come along with a crazy idea and he has got you upset. Get a hold on your imagination. Please. It's over now and I would like to forget. Let it be over. Please, Felicia."

Felicia came to the table and dropped heavily into a chair. She nodded two or three times before she spoke, and her voice was low and controlled.

"I suppose you are right. It is merely that I am confused when I see that you are lying."

"I'm sorry. I saw no harm in it."

Half the time she had been lying to herself, she thought. She wished she could be as sure as she pretended to be that Eduardo's death was an accident. Even if it was not, she supposed, there would be no change in her plans. Not if she wanted to live. And there would be little change in her feelings, she admitted. She did not miss Eduardo or owe him vengeance or anything like that. She had fallen out of love with him as soon as she had got to know him for the small soul that he was. A small soul who would do anything for money—even share his wife.

He had been well paid for his hospitality and the sanctuary of the high, remote cabin. Fifty dollars in gold every month, plus the cost of supplies. He had kept the money in a quart jar under his bunk. When he was dead and the two men were leaving, they had taken the jar with almost eight hundred dollars in it. They had instructed Susanna very carefully as to what she was to do. Then they had given her ten twenty-dollar gold pieces.

"That'll be enough to bury him and buy you a stage ticket," Slip Ambrose had said. "It would look suspicious for a young widow to have much cash. We'll keep the rest of this till you join us."

The deputy's office was in a small stone building with the jail at the back. Zack Mayberly lounged beside the deputy's desk, facing the doorway. The deputy sat behind the desk, filing his fingernails. He was a cherubic little person with the best-kept fingernails Mayberly had ever seen on a man.

"Now wouldn't that be something?" the deputy said. "Scipio and Tucker Ambrose holed up right under my nose and I let 'em slip away." He clearly considered the possibility remote.

"Tell me about Susanna Velasquez," Mayberly said.

"Well, I happen to know a little bit about her. She came here with her grandfather when she was about ten years old. He was a harness maker and a saddle maker, a good one but old and slow. He made quality saddles for folks who could pay for 'em. The sheriff has one of his saddles and swears by it. Well, the old man had no control over the girl and she grew up wild. He died before she was seven-

7

teen and she married Eduardo Velasquez. He had just
built that cabin up on Grizzly Creek and he was catching
wild horses and breaking them. That is one hell of a way to
make a living and he didn't do well at it. He was banged up
most of the time. He brought down two or three horses
every couple of months or so. Got maybe twenty-five
dollars apiece for 'em. Anyhow, it wasn't long before we
heard there was two prospectors up there with him and
Susanna. It never occurred to anybody that they might be
hiding out.''

"Doc tells me Susanna got herself beaten up a couple of
times.''

"He treated her a couple of times, so it could have
happened more often. First time, she insisted she fell off a
horse. Second time was bad. She lost a baby, dang near
died. She admitted to being beat up that time. Said
Eduardo did it, but she wouldn't press charges.''

"You never saw anything of the two prospectors?''

"Well, the one called Dyer came into town once, threw
a hell of a bender. Busted out dang near every window on
whorehouse row. I collared him, put him in jail. Next day
Eduardo showed up with damage money and that was the
end of it.''

"Dyer was a small man?''

"Real small. Now don't go telling me I might have had
Tucker Ambrose in a cell.''

"Tucker is a wild drinker. A real whisky head. Sip's a
drinker, too, but not as bad. He likes to beat up women.''

"I'll be danged,'' the deputy said. "You figure they're
gone for good?''

"Seems likely.''

The deputy looked relieved. "What you plan to do
next?''

"Hang around and hope for a lead. Seems like there's a chance the girl might head for the new hide-out, wherever it is."

"I'm danged if I see how you figure that."

"Just a hunch."

The deputy gave a nervous little shrug. "Suit yourself."

Mayberly left the office and strolled down Dos Pinos' sleepy street. It was warm for April in this high country. The storekeeper, who was also the postmaster, sat in front of the general store, puffing on a pipe and getting a touch of sun. He returned Mayberly's nod and got up and followed him inside. Mayberly stopped at a wired-off area just inside the door. There was a window in the wire and above it gold letters spelled out *U.S. Post Office.*

"Mail isn't in yet," the storekeeper said.

"I need a favor," Mayberly said. "If Susanna Velasquez gets a letter I'd like to know about it. There's no regulation against your taking note of a postmark or a return address, is there?"

"There might be one about passing that kind of information along. I don't know exactly. The Post Office Department—"

Mayberly took a five-dollar gold piece from his purse and pushed it through the window. The storekeeper stared at it, pocketed it, and grinned.

"Come to think about it, I don't remember any such regulation."

"I'll be stopping by every day after the mail is in," Mayberly said.

He crossed the street to the small hotel where he was staying, which was also the stage station. Sizing up his man, he laid a silver dollar on the desk in front of the clerk.

9

"If Susanna Velasquez buys a stage ticket, I'd like you to get word to me."

"Sure thing," the clerk said.

He waited for most of a week before a lead came, such as it was. It came from neither the storekeeper nor the clerk but from the deputy, who beckoned Mayberly into his office one afternoon after the stage was in. He had a telegram.

"It was sent to the sheriff at the county seat," he said. "Had to be relayed through Cheyenne, Denver, and Colorado Springs. We got no telegraph here, I guess you know that. Anyhow, the sheriff knows you're here and he sent it down on the stage with a note for me to give it to you. It's from the sheriff at Castle Rock, South Dakota."

2

A DEATH-DRY buzzing sounded from inside the root house as Melody Coates pushed open the door. She sprang backward reflexively. The rattlesnake was coiled to the left of the door and struck at its edge as it swung open.

Melody found herself running toward the ranch house, screaming. She halted as the boy came out of the house. He snatched up the hoe that stood beside the door and hurried past her to the root house.

"Be careful, Stevie. It's just inside the doorway. Be careful."

The boy was nine years old, but he would be careful. He wouldn't admit it, but he was as scared of snakes as she was. Being male, he suppressed terror and—carefully— played the role of protector.

She watched from a distance while he skillfully killed the snake, teasing it into striking at the hoe and then chopping fast and hard. Then there was the ritual of scooping a hole in the hard South Dakota soil and burying the head. After that he cut off the rattles with his pocketknife and buried the body. He came toward her shaking the rattles.

"Eight and a button," he said.

"You suppose there's another around?" she said. They both knew there probably was. The snakes came from a prairie-dog town the other side of the creek. They usually came in pairs.

"I'll look around," Stevie said. His cheeks were pale.

"Be careful," she said.

He went back to the root house and stood for a time in the doorway. Probing ahead with the hoe, he went inside. He struck a match and lit the candle they kept beside the door. For a long two or three minutes Melody watched its small flame moving about inside. Stevie came out, shaking his head.

"Nothing in there."

That was a relief. A nine-year-old with a hoe could dispatch a rattler in the open without much risk, even a big rattler. In the crowded dark confines of the root house, the danger would have been greater.

She steeled herself and went into the root house. She quickly gathered big gnarled carrots and an onion in her apron and took the last jar of canned peas from a shelf. She crossed the yard to the small, unpainted, weather-grayed house and went into the kitchen. She washed the carrots and began to dice them. She had soaked a pint of barley overnight and she had a beef bone simmering and would make soup. It would be thick and nourishing, but Stevie wouldn't eat much of it. Snake killing always diminished his appetite. She crossed the small room to a window and saw him moving slowly into a patch of short dry grass not far from the root house, hoe ready.

She had had him four years now, since he was five and she eighteen. Dad had been alive when Martha had turned up with him. They had been in Wyoming then, renting a few acres and raising hogs and potatoes and a few sheep. They hadn't seen Martha since she had eloped with Sip Ambrose. Dad hadn't approved of Sip and had told her

12

she couldn't see him, and she had just picked up and run off with him. They had had a few letters from her, telling about Stevie. The letters came from half a dozen different towns and she never gave a return address. She seemed to be on the move all the time. After a while they knew why. It was in the papers.

Sip Ambrose and his brother Tucker were wanted for bank robbery in Colorado Springs. A week later they were arrested in Trinidad and broke jail. After that their list of crimes grew steadily. Alamosa, Durango, Denver, Colorado Springs again. Stage robbery, bank robbery, murder. At last, without warning, Martha had arrived with the boy.

Her nose was broken and she was missing some teeth and had some broken ribs. There was something else wrong with her, too, something deep and painful that the doctor was never certain about. She got a little better for a time, but when winter came her body just seemed to give up.

"I want to live," she said. "For Stevie. If I could last till spring, I think I might make it. But I'm not going to, Melody. You and Dad will have to take the boy. Keep him away from Sip."

She had died the last day of February, leaving a written request that Dad be made the boy's guardian. The next year Dad had put the sheep out on the range too early in the spring. He had got lost in a late blizzard trying to save them. When a search party brought him in, he had pneumonia. He sank into a coma and was dead within twenty-four hours.

A few months later, rumors reached Melody that a stranger had been asking questions about Martha and Stevie. A big stranger who fitted Sip Ambrose's descrip-

13

tion. Melody had sold the hogs and what was left of the sheep. Without telling anyone where they were going, she had brought Stevie to this remote corner of South Dakota. She had rented this small and rickety house from the bank at Castle Rock for ten dollars a month. It was on a broken-down farm a mile out of town, and Mr. Gibbs, the banker, raised hay on the rest of the property. She kept a cow, a horse, a few chickens. She made her living as a dressmaker.

She was good at it and she kept fairly busy. She charged ten cents an hour and sometimes she made a small profit on material that she ordered from Chicago. She patronized the local dry-goods store most of the time, however. She had a sort of agreement with the proprietor, who recommended her to the ladies of the community. He had been a big help to her, especially at first.

Soon after she arrived, she had talked with the county sheriff. She told him frankly that Sip Ambrose was Stevie's father. It seemed the prudent thing to do at the time, although she regretted it now. She had asked him to keep her secret, but he had said he ought to tell his deputies and the Castle Rock town marshal. If there was any danger of Sip showing up, she would be safer if they were alerted, the sheriff said. He assured her that the deputies and the marshall could be trusted. But within a week everybody knew that she was Sip Ambrose's sister-in-law and the boy was his son. Worse, the story had got twisted. There were those who said that she herself had been Ambrose's woman and that Stevie was her child.

She was not ostracized. People were friendly enough, but it was a dutiful friendliness. She was seldom invited anywhere. Her customers sometimes asked prying questions, but she had not one single friend whom she felt she could talk to intimately. The young men of the community never came calling. Not the Coates gal, boys. Ambrose will show up some day. If you happen to be around, bucko, you're apt to get a bellyful of lead.

She knew she should move on to a new place, for Stevie's sake as well as her own. She planned to do it someday, when she got a few dollars ahead. But at ten cents an hour, that was a dream. It was all she could do to pay the rent.

She got the vegetables and the barley into the pot and left it to simmer. She crossed to the window again. Stevie was working his way along the pasture fence toward the barn. He was being careful, scanning the ground and poking the hoe into the tufts of tall grass at the bases of the fence posts. He kept the hoe filed razor-sharp and it was a good weapon. He had sense enough not to go under the barn or anything like that. Or into the hayfield. He would search the open ground around the house and the barn and if he didn't find the rattler he would quit. Melody went into the parlor, where she had laid out green silk on the table and pinned a pattern to it. She began to cut out a dress for Mrs. Gibbs, the banker's wife.

Stevie found the snake behind the barn, sliding through a clump of cornflowers, coiling instantly when it saw that it couldn't get away from him, sounding off as he approached with the hoe raised. It knew it was going to die, he guessed. It struck at the hoe and he chopped hard and then it struck at itself, at the wound the hoe had made. He got it behind the head and bore down and beheaded it. Killing was an ugly thing, especially killing snakes. He dragged the head away from the slowly writhing body with the hoe and scooped out a six-inch hole and buried the

15

head. He got out his knife and put his foot on the snake just above the rattles and cut them off. Then he buried the body. He could sell the rattles for ten cents to the proprietor of the Happy Hour, who had a collection of them mounted on a velvet-covered board on the back bar.

When the burying was done, he looked up and was startled to see a stranger watching him. He was only ten yards away, sitting on a big sorrel horse with the barn squarely between him and the house.

"Howdy, boy. Whyn't you skin that snake? Snakeskin makes a pretty hatband."

Stevie found that he had raised the hoe defensively. Embarrassed, he lowered it. The man swung down off the horse and came closer. He was big and solid and dirty-looking. His face was covered with black stubble. His eyes were pale and glassy blue.

"I don't like to skin things," the boy said. "It's messy. Besides, my aunt wouldn't like snakeskins around."

"Your aunt's name Melody Coates?"

"Yes, sir."

"You Stephen Ambrose?"

"Yes, sir."

"Your aunt in the house?"

"Yes, sir."

The man jerked his head toward the big sorrel, grazing a few feet behind him. "What you think of that horse? He's a beauty, ain't he?"

Stevie nodded. The man had put himself squarely in his way. He considered turning and going around the barn in the other direction.

"You like a ride on him?"

"I got to get back to the house," Stevie said.

"He's got a lot of spirit. You think you can handle

him?''

"I got to get back.'' Stevie turned and started the long way around the barn. The man strode after him and got in front of him.

"You figured out who I am, ain't you?''

"I think so.''

"Well, least you can do is shake hands with me.''

The boy shifted the hoe and took the man's extended hand. The man held on firmly, grinning when Stevie tried to pull away.

"Now you tell me who I am,'' the man said.

"I reckon you're my father,'' Stevie said.

Melody finished cutting out the dress and gathered up the scraps. She looked out the window and didn't see the boy. She went into the kitchen and tasted the soup, then she went to the door and called him and got no answer. She circled the house and saw nothing of him. Still calling, she walked around the barn and found the hoe in back of it. She knew something was wrong then, even before she found the faint hoofmarks and the big boot tracks on the hard soil.

She went into the barn and got a bridle on the horse. She didn't take time to harness it and hitch it to the buckboard but climbed onto its back and rode it out of the barn and headed for town.

The sheriff, a round-faced, bulb-bottomed handshaker with an eye to his political future, was visibly excited. He got off some telegrams and then, with a deputy, rode out for a look at the ground. He took all the coffee and bacon and bread Melody had in the house and set out to follow the tracks. He and the deputy were gone for three days.

17

In the meantime the news spread. At least a dozen neighbors dropped in to console her—and to ask questions. They tried to be kind. Men did her chores for her. Women brought pies and cakes. Two or three suggested that she ought to come and stay with them for a few days. They seemed relieved when she declined. Mr. Gibbs insisted on lending her a shotgun. She took it, although she didn't see much sense to it. If Sip Ambrose had wanted to harm her, he had his opportunity. He wouldn't be back.

The sheriff and deputy returned with nothing substantial to report.

"The tracks lead from here to Five-Mile Creek," the sheriff said. "Two other horses were waiting there. Assuming it was Sip Ambrose who took the boy, it's a fair guess that his brother Tucker met him with an extra horse. They took the stage road west for a few miles. Then they took to open country. We lost the trail in a patch of badlands. It's a fair guess they crossed into Wyoming. I've sent telegrams to most every county seat in Wyoming and Colorado. There's nothing to do but be patient, Miss Coates. There's seventy-five hundred dollars apiece on the Ambrose brothers' heads. They have a reputation that reaches from here to kingdom come. Any lawman would give his eyeteeth to bring them in. They will eventually be taken. You'll get the boy back."

A week later there was no further news. Melody had her fill of being patient. She sold the horse and the cow and the chickens and the buckboard. She studied a map and decided it was likely that the Ambrose brothers had passed through the town of Beulah, just over the Wyoming line. She bought a stage ticket.

The sheriff and Mr. Gibbs did their best to discourage her. They pointed out that she had no plan, no clue, not

18

even a solid hunch. Even if, for a miracle, she dug up some sort of lead at Beulah, the trail would be cold by this time. And if she persisted in a search that should be left to the law, she was likely to wind up broke and alone in a town full of strangers.

And they were right.

She spent two days in and around Beulah, questioning merchants, cowhands, loafers—practically everyone she met. No one had seen anything of two men traveling with a boy. She went on to other towns, working toward the Colorado border. Sundance. Upton. Osage. Douglas. Wheatland. After two weeks of traveling, she found herself in a Laramie hotel room, sitting out a driving rainstorm. She had four dollars and sixty cents in her purse and no idea of what she was going to do next.

She sat at the window and watched the rain beat against the buildings of the town and glisten on the boardwalks and gather in swirling coffee-colored puddles in the deserted street. After a time, a poncho-draped man rode into town from the north, a big man on a big, slogging horse. He rode with head bowed against the rain, hatbrim hiding his face. He reached the livery barn and disappeared into its huge dark entrance. He seemed to Melody to have been part of the storm, a fleeting phenomenon bred of wind and weather.

He was a long time in the barn. He was rubbing down his horse, she supposed. Then he came up the boardwalk on the far side of the street, large and dark and shapeless in the poncho. He crossed toward the hotel, taking huge strides in the mud. When he was just below her window, he turned his face upward in the rain and saw her. It was a hard lean face but not so old as she had expected. He smiled at her in the rain and seemed suddenly boyish and

19

friendly. She quickly turned her head and did not smile back, but she was cheered by the incident and took strength from it.

Five minutes later there was a knock on her door. She opened it and he was there, minus hat and poncho.

"My name is Mayberly," he said. "Are you Melody Coates?"

3

SHE ACKNOWLEDGED that she was Melody Coates and stepped back so he could come into the room. She closed the door and was immediately annoyed by her lack of propriety. He walked to the window and looked up and down the street before he turned to face her.

"I heard about the boy disappearing," he said. "I went to Castle Rock to talk to you, but you'd left. Been trailing you clear across Wyoming."

"You know something about Stevie?"

"No, ma'am. I'm hunting the Ambrose boys. It seems like you might be onto something that would help."

She sat down on the bed, sighing. "I'm not onto anything at all the authorities don't know. It seemed to me they weren't trying hard enough. I was going crazy waiting for news that didn't come, so I struck out for myself. I've been going from town to town asking questions. I've gotten exactly nowhere and I'm feeling very foolish. Are you a lawman, Mr. Mayberly?"

"No, ma'am."

He moved the chair away from the window and sat down. She thought she detected a weariness in the act, a disappointment. He grinned at her and the impression was gone.

21

"The next question is usually 'Are you a Pinkerton man?' " he said. "The answer to that is no too. I'm just a greedy hunter after the reward money. I've been trying to run down the Ambrose boys for four years. A couple of times I've been just a jump behind them. Most of the time it's been a pretty cold trail."

"I can't help you, Mr. Mayberly. I don't mean to be snippy. I just don't have any clues."

"Your sister was with you when she died. Seems like she might have mentioned something that would help—a hide-out, an alias her husband used, something like that."

"If she said anything like that, I've forgotten it. She died more than three years ago. She didn't hide out with Sip—at least not after Stevie was born. He left her alone for months at a time. She was watched, of course, but he managed to see her when he wanted to. He brought money and beat her up, she said."

"Have you ever seen the Ambrose brothers?"

"I saw Sip once or twice before Martha married him. I wasn't more than twelve years old."

"Would you know him now?"

"I think so."

"Describe him for me."

"You've never seen him?"

"No, ma'am. Matter of fact, it's hard to find people who've actually seen either of their faces. They always wear masks when they pull a holdup. I think I've pieced together pretty good pictures of the two of them, but I'm still piecing. You might be able to add something."

"I doubt it. I remember nothing distinctive—except maybe his light blue eyes. He was big. Tall and solid.

Dark hair. He had a heavy beard that gave his face a dark look even when he was freshly shaved. He'd be about thirty-eight years old now. That's all I remember.''

"That's pretty good. You never saw Tucker?"

"Not that I remember."

"They're half brothers, you know. Tucker has some Indian blood."

"Yes. Martha mentioned that. She said he walked like an Indian—slightly pigeon-toed."

"You're doing fine, Miss Coates. Maybe if we can just keep rambling on, you'll remember other things. Do you mind?"

"Not a bit."

He got to his feet, fishing a big Raymond watch from a vest pocket and cupping it in his hand. "The dining room should be open. Will you join me for dinner?"

The suddenness of the invitation caught her off guard. In an effort to conserve her dwindling cash, she had been living mostly on cheese and crackers that she ate in her room. It came to her that he might know this. He had been trailing her from town to town and he had probably been questioning hotel clerks about her. If that was so, if he was being kind, she resented it. But he was already moving toward the door, taking it for granted that she would accept.

"I'll meet you in the dining room," he said. "Ten minutes?"

"That will be fine," she said.

When he had gone, she went to the window and saw that the rain had almost stopped. Off to the west there was a break in the ash-colored sky and distant peaks stood gold-rimmed against a band of pink and blue. When she turned away, the room seemed very dark and she lighted a lamp. She stood before the mirror over the washstand and found that she was smiling. She wondered how long it had been since she had smiled except in a polite, deliberate way. She had come to think of herself as a purpose rather than a person. It was nice to stand in front of a mirror and be a girl who was going to have dinner with a man. Her hair had a red-gold cast in the lamplight. It was really sort of pretty....

They dined on tenderloin steaks, baked potatoes, and an assortment of vegetables. And fresh-baked bread and pale sweet butter and fragrant coffee and for dessert there were fresh strawberries with honey-thick cream. They talked about the Ambrose brothers in an easy, sort of gossipy way. Melody managed to recall that Sip had nice teeth and a good singing voice. And that Tucker had a mangled ear.

"Martha told me about that," she explained. "Tucker bought a throwing knife from a Chinese gambler and he carried it in a sheath sewed inside the back of his shirt just below the collar. The idea, of course, was that he could reach to the back of his neck, grab the handle, and throw the knife in a flash without any wasted motion. Well, he was practicing one time when he was drunk and he sliced his ear in two...."

She found herself laughing aloud, giggling almost. It was as if all the drab determination of the past weeks had been balanced by a secret build-up of silliness sealed away in some deep corner of herself till it was near the bursting point.

"It isn't really funny, I guess."

Mayberly was grinning. "You have no idea how beautiful you are when you laugh."

Their eyes met and she quickly sobered. He was a good-looking man, she thought. In a rather battered way, of course. His nose had been broken—more than once, she guessed—and there was a small white scar high on his left cheek. After all, he was a—bounty hunter was the term. Under the poise and the nice manners, he was very likely a beast.

"Now I'm going to be flustered," she said. "You've no idea how long it's been since a man paid me a compliment. Are you buttering me up for something?" It had never in her life occurred to her that that phrase might have a coarse implication. Now she was suddenly struck by the possibility that it might, and she was truly flustered. "I'm tired and I've eaten too much and I guess I'm not making much sense. I'm trying to say it's all been very nice. The dinner and someone to talk with—you can't imagine how much I've enjoyed it."

"Matter of fact, I was thinking of making a suggestion," Mayberly said. "First, I want to ask a question. You're determined to go on with this blind search of yours?"

"Yes, Mr. Mayberly. It's blind and discouraging. I'm going to have to stop and work in order to support myself. But I'm going on to Colorado and I'm going on from town to town in the hope of hearing something. Maybe it will take years. But I have to try. I can't give up."

Mayberly nodded grimly. "Now for my suggestion.

It seems like we might be of help to each other, Miss Coates. I've got a small lead in a little town in Colorado called Dos Pinos. I left there when I heard your nephew had been kidnaped. I hoped there might be a trail to follow. Since there isn't, I'm going back to Dos Pinos. If I should get onto something there, it seems like we might work together."

"I'll help any way I can, of course. But I don't see how I'd be much good to you."

"I probably know as much about the Ambrose brothers as anyone alive," he said. "But I've never seen them. I could pass either of them in the street and never know him. You'd recognize Sip. You'd know the boy a hundred yards away. If I get a trail to follow, I'd like to take you with me. It will be a sort of partnership. If you come across a lead, you'll let me know. And no one else. I won't share any reward money with you. Understand that. If you'll agree to those terms, I'll help out with your expenses."

He was leaning forward on his elbows and so was she. She studied his face as he talked and she was frightened. Frightened of herself, of what might happen to her if she threw in with this strong man who seemed so frank and decent and who probably could not be trusted.

"There's another thing you ought to know," he said. "If you get close to Sip and he knows it, he may try to kill you. I may count on that and use you for bait."

She laughed uneasily. "You lay it on the line, Mr. Mayberly. I'll say that for you."

"I'd expect as much from you. For one thing, I'd want your word that you'll leave decisions up to me. I

26

don't want you calling in the law unless I agree."

"I don't know about *that*. If Stevie were endangered in any way—"

"Naturally, the boy comes first. I'll agree to that."

"I don't know. I—I wish I knew more about you, Mr. Mayberly."

"Will it help if I say this is strictly a business arrangement? I'll do nothing to make things awkward for you as a woman."

She smiled. "That's a quaint way of putting it, Mr. Mayberly. But I appreciate it. I'm almost persuaded, but I think I'd better sleep on it."

"Sure. But whatever you decide, go around town tomorrow and ask your questions. Act exactly as you would if you had turned me down."

"Oh? We're to keep any deal we make a secret?"

"Yes, ma'am. Also you're not to mention Dos Pinos to anybody. Now I'm going to touch your knee under the table, Miss Coates. Don't jump. I'm not getting fresh, I'm putting a fifty-dollar bill in your lap."

She felt the slight movement of his hand. Her fingers found the folded bill. "Mr. Mayberly—"

"No protesting, please. If you decide we're not partners, you can give it back to me. Now I would like you to pretend to give me a quick and final brush off."

"I don't understand."

"Pretend that I've insulted you and that you wouldn't think of making an agreement with me. Look angry and get up and walk out."

"You sound as if someone is watching us."

"Yes, ma'am. Don't look around the room. Look angry and start talking and get up in the middle of a sentence and go straight up to your room.''

"I'll try."

"Don't smile."

"I'm not."

"Your eyes are smiling. Look stern."

She met his eyes and held them, trying to look stern and to think of something to say. She drew herself up indignantly and began in an icy, barely audible voice. Strangely enough, the words came easily.

"You're very persuasive, Mr. Mayberly. You tell me what to do and I seem to do it. I'm not always so easygoing. I'm weak enough and desperate enough to take your money, so I guess we're going to be partners, as you put it. You're a professional man hunter. It's plain you'd do most anything for money. I don't think I trust you very much. The first time you lie to me or act in bad faith, I'm going to drop you like a hot tomato—I mean potato—and you're going to be sorry you ever saw me." She stood up, raising her voice now, and said, "Good night, Mr. Mayberly!"

He got belatedly to his feet, as if caught unaware, and watched her trot out of the dining room. He followed to the doorway and paused there as she crossed the lobby and hurried up the stairs. There was a conviction to her performance that both pleased and annoyed him.

He turned from the doorway and sat down at the nearest table. There was a lean, stoop-shouldered man at the table, hunched over a bowl of soup. He had very heavy black eyebrows and a thin mustache that hooked around the corners of his mouth to join his small, sculptured beard. He wore a pale doeskin coat with red-and-white beading over the pockets. His name, Mayberly knew, was Harry Yadkin.

"You've been trailing her," Mayberly said.

"So've you, looks like. Looks like you got your wings clipped too. I could have told you she wouldn't go for sweet talk. She needs any help, she'll call the law."

"You swore to me you were going to stay off the Ambrose boys, Harry."

"That was after I got shot up down at Stonewall. You was mad enough to finish the job and I was in no shape to argue."

"You shot a horse out from under me, Harry. If you'd taken the Ambrose boys and collected the reward, I'd have killed you."

"That was Shultz dropped your horse, not me. He done you a favor. If him and me couldn't take the Ambroses, how could you have done it alone?"

"I'd have played it smarter than you did. You rode smack into an ambush."

"That was Shultz's fault, rest his stupid Dutch soul. He figured they went south around Culebra Peak. Said we should go north and be waitin' for 'em on the other side. But they was waitin' for us. Shultz got a buffalo slug clean through him, never knew what hit him. I caught two .44s. Crawled into some rocks where I could make a stand. They knew I was hit and no more danger to 'em, so they didn't take the time to flush me out. I made it to that mining camp where you found me. Shape I was in, naturally I agreed to lay off the Ambroses or anything else you wanted. Jesus, you was mad."

"Now you've changed your mind?"

"Looks like it, don't it?"

"The Ambrose brothers are my kill, Harry. I'll run over anybody who gets in my way."

Yadkin pushed the soup bowl to one side, using the back of his hand. "There's no rules to this game, Mayberly. Don't try to make any. Anyways, I've been following the woman for a week. If anybody's poaching, looks like it's you."

"All right, Harry. Follow her to hell and back—she's all yours. Just don't ever follow me again. You do, and *I'll* bushwhack *you* this time. And I won't aim at the horse."

Yadkin considered this, tracing the precise outline of his beard with a fingertip. "Looks like you figure she's just fumbling around, going noplace. I about decided the same thing. You got something else?"

"Not a damn thing," Mayberly said quickly, aware of Yadkin's veiled, poker-table appraisal. "I'm going to ride out of here tomorrow and start over."

"You've got something, you're going to need help."

"I do, I'll make a deal with the law or I'll hire somebody by the day. I'm not sharing that bounty with anybody."

"Greedy," Yadkin said. "I happen to pass your grave, I'll say, 'There lies a greedy dead man.' "

Mayberly got to his feet. "It'll be the other way around, you ever follow me again."

He went into the lobby and across it to the registration desk. He asked the clerk for a Union Pacific timetable, a sheet of paper, and an envelope. He climbed the stairs to his room, where he studied the timetable for a while and then composed a note to Melody Coates.

Miss Coates:

Go about your questioning in the morning as we agreed. If you notice somebody watching you, pay no attention to him. At 1:30 check out of the hotel. Go to the railroad station and buy a ticket to Cheyenne. There is an eastbound train due at 2:10. Take it. It is due in Cheyenne at 3:35. There is a connecting train to Denver scheduled for 4 o'clock. It waits if your train is late. Buy a ticket to Denver but get off at Fort Collins. Check in at the Rocky Mountain Hotel. Register as Mrs. George Russell. Keep out of sight and be patient. Wait till you hear from me.

I ask you to do this in order to shake off a man who has been trailing you. I'll have him out of the way when you leave Laramie, and once you have a day's start, you will be hard to trace.

> *Respectfully,*
> *Z. Mayberly*

He found the corridor empty. He quickly walked down it to Melody Coates's door, slid the letter under it, and returned to his room.

4

MAYBERLY SLEPT late the next morning. He bathed and shaved and went to the dining room for a large and leisurely breakfast. He returned to his room then, a corner room with a big bay window. He sat for an hour with his feet on the sill, watching the town's street and enjoying a cigar.

The day was bright and mild and the street was active with the unhurried commerce of a small town. Mayberly glimpsed Melody Coates at the far end of it near the sheriff's office. Later he watched her work her way down the far side, going from store to store, no doubt asking the questions she had asked in other towns. He saw nothing of Harry Yadkin.

When he had finished the cigar, he packed his saddlebags and went down to the desk to check out. There were several loungers in the lobby, but Yadkin was not among them. Neither was he in the dining room or the bar. Mayberly went into the street and down it to the livery stable, still seeing no sign of the man and thinking that he was probably watching from a hotel window or some other concealed vantage point. In any case, Mayberly was reasonably certain that he wouldn't leave town without Yadkin observing him.

He paid the stableman, saddled his horse, and rode south out of town. Half a mile along, he left the road and circled back northward. His route took him to high ground east of the town. When he was opposite it, he left his horse in a ravine and climbed to where he could look down on the clustered rooftops, the looping river, the railroad, the road. There was a solitary rider on the road south of town, already nearing the place where Mayberly had turned off. He rode with a forward slope to his shoulders and he wore a pale coat. Mayberly waited till he swung away from the road, plainly following hoofmarks that were deep and distinct after yesterday's rain. Yadkin had taken the bait.

Mayberly remounted and continued his ride, staying east of the road till he was well past the town. Then he angled into it and continued northward.

The road and the railroad followed the swerving line of the Laramie River, marked by trees and a tangle of brush. The rest of the country was largely barren except for its dappling of sage and occasional small soddy patches of yellow-green grass. It was cattle country, not much good for anything else without irrigation. Somebody had once figured out that it took twenty-odd acres of this sort of pasture to support one cow. It was a land of huge ranges with ranch houses few and far between.

Mayberly looked back occasionally and saw no sign of pursuit. That was as he expected. Yadkin would keep his distance and take pains not to show himself. That time down near Stonewall, Mayberly had no suspicion he was being trailed until Yadkin and his partner had got ahead of him and done for his horse.

He stayed with the road for the better part of an hour, meeting a man and a woman in a spring wagon and an old man on a mule. He forded the river then and pointed west toward low barren foothills with Medicine Bow Peak rising hazily forty miles away. He had worked in this country as a kid and the lay of it came back to him as he got deeper into it. It was uneven country, sometimes gently rising, sometimes cut by draws and scarred by sheer-sided ridges. There was a lake to the north, he remembered, and a long, creek-streaked valley to the south. He avoided these and chose a course not likely to take him close to human dwelling places.

In the middle of the afternoon he came to a spring in a green little ravine with a stand of pine on the far slope. It would do, he decided. He watered his horse and then rode a slanting course up the slope, skirting the trees. When he was past them, he turned back and rode straight into the grove. Deep in its shelter, he dismounted and tied the horse. Pulling his Winchester from its boot, he walked to the edge of the trees and sat down behind a little screen of saplings.

He had only a short wait. Yadkin jogged into sight at the lower end of the ravine and reined up. He paused there a time, a furlong away, scanning the spring, the grove, the surrounding hills. At last he came on, the horse slogging in wet turf as it neared the spring.

Yadkin dismounted to let the animal drink, tasted the water himself, filled his canteen. Then he lifted himself into the saddle and swung up the hill toward the grove, following the tracks Mayberly had left. Mayberly waited until he had passed. Then he rose from behind the curtain of young pines and stepped into the open. He leveled the Winchester.

"Yadkin!"

Yadkin swung his horse around and halted. He pressed his lips into an uneasy grin. "Skin me for a snared coon. Looks like I walked right into it."

"Get down easy, Harry. Keep that right hand in sight."

Yadkin gave a little toss of his head and obeyed. At Mayberly's instruction he unbuckled his gunbelt, dropped it, moved to the base of a tree, and sat down.

"You used to carry a Henry D. in your boot," Mayberly said. "Shuck 'em."

Yadkin gave him a long look of sullen protest and pulled off his boots. Mayberly extracted a derringer from a small buckskin holster sewed inside the right one.

"Now empty your pockets."

Yadkin produced a pocketknife, a bandanna, a buckskin purse with a drawstring. Mayberly picked up the purse and opened it. It contained two folded twenty-dollar bills and some gold and some silver coins. He closed the purse and slipped it into a pocket of his trousers. Yadkin glared indignantly.

"You ain't going to rob me?"

"You owe me for a horse, Harry."

"I've seen some mean things—"

"Shut up. I told you I'd kill you if you followed me again. I may decide to do it."

There was a deep and dangerous hatred in Yadkin's look. Then he grinned again.

"You've got a lesson to learn," Mayberly said. "I'm gambling that you're smart enough to learn it. If there's a next time, I won't gamble again. I'll stop you for good. Put on your boots. You've got a long walk."

He uncinched Yadkin's saddle and flung it off the horse. He drew the Winchester from the saddle boot and, squatting, worked the lever till the magazine was empty. He scooped up the shells and stuffed them into his pockets.

"I'll leave your saddle and guns. You can cache 'em and come back for 'em. I'm taking your ammunition."

Besides the .44s in Yadkin's gunbelt, Mayberly found two boxes in the man's saddlebags. There was also a box of .30-caliber rim-fire shells for the derringer. Mayberly pocketed them all.

"Town of McFadden's about ten miles north northwest," he said. "You better get started if you're going to make it by dark."

Yadkin stashed the saddle among the saplings, tying the tops of several together to protect it from the weather. He picked up saddlebags, canteen, and guns and without another word strode down the slope and northward across the ravine.

Mayberly transferred his saddle to Yadkin's horse and continued westward, leading his own animal. After a few minutes, he swung south, riding hard, cantering when the ground was good. By nightfall he reached the Laramie River at a point several miles south of the town. He camped on its bank and was on his way again at first light.

He followed the winding course of the river, stopping at the town of Jelm for a breakfast of pancakes and bacon. Before midmorning, he judged he was over the Colorado line. At noon, he rested an hour. Then he put his saddle on his own horse and turned Yadkin's loose. He left the river and bore westward into high, rugged country and the going was slow until he hit a stage road. He reached a stage station shortly before sundown and decided to take the night here. If he got an early start, he would be in Dos Pinos by noon the next day.

The station was run by a widow and her son. It consisted of a series of fenced pastures, a huge barn, and a square house with a roofed porch all the way around it. The widow explained that the northbound stage was due in half an hour and that supper would be on the table when it arrived. When the passengers had eaten, the coach would go on another twenty miles to the next station, where they would spend the night.

The pump was on the barn side of the house. There were benches on the porch on that side with mirrors above them and washbasins, soap, and towels laid out for the stage passengers. Mayberly washed up and then sank into a chair on the front part of the porch to smoke a cigar and wait for supper.

The stage strained into sight at the crest of a spur to the southwest and rocked down the road to the station. It made the turn in swirling dust, pinkish in the sun's afterglow, and halted in front of the barn. The coach doors butterflied and passengers climbed out, filing toward the outhouses behind the station. There were seven of them, five men and two women. One of the women was plump and matronly. The other, trim in an ankle-length skirt and short jacket, was young and dark-haired. Mayberly scanned her with idle appreciation and then suddenly recognized her. Susanna Velasquez.

She hadn't seen him. He waited until she disappeared around the building; then he went into the station. He made arrangements with the widow to have his dinner brought to his room. He told her simply that there was a stage passenger he wanted to avoid, and a silver dollar sealed the bargain. She also agreed to ask the stage driver to pay a visit to Mayberly's room.

The widow's son, a silent boy barely out of his teens, brought Mayberly's dinner. Mulligan stew, bread, coffee, and cake with a gritty sugar frosting. Mayberly was eating the cake when the driver knocked on the door. He was a young man with a pointed blond beard and he wore a fringed buckskin jacket. He seemed to be trying for the dash and glamor of an earlier generation of stage drivers.

"You want to see me, sport?"

"The name is Mayberly. Have a chair."

"Just as soon stand. Been bouncing my butt on that coach all day. What's on your mind, Mr. Mayberry?"

A city boy, Mayberly decided. He had learned to drive a six-horse hitch and had fixed himself up like General Custer, but he still had the peculiar defensive arrogance of Kansas City or Chicago. Mayberly picked up his saddlebags from the bed and fished out a letter, which he handed to the driver. It was written on Bell & Tovey Stage and Express stationery and was signed by H. B. Tovey. The driver was impressed in spite of himself.

"If this is genuine, you're Zack Mayberly and you're to be extended 'extraordinary co-operation.' You hitting me for a ride, is that it?"

"I want information about one of your passengers. The dark-haired girl—Susanna Velasquez. Where is she going?"

The man scowled at the letter again. He looked up

with a new friendliness. "Zack Mayberly. You the man who used to run that seventy-mile line between Bramble and the Lucky Cut?"

"I am."

"I made the connection at Bramble a couple times myself. You know Sid Myers?"

"The chicken farmer? Used to ship eggs to Durango."

"Still does." The driver grinned. "I guess you get extraordinary co-operation. The girl got on at Dos Pinos. She had a ticket to Fort Collins, but she asked me to change it for her. Wants to get to Spinnerville."

"Spinnerville?"

"Spinnerville, Montana. I never been there myself."

"She's in for a long trip."

"Two days to Casper. She'll have to lay over there. Then she'll have another two days and a couple of changes before she gets over the Montana line."

That was interesting, Mayberly thought. Nobody had suspected that the Ambrose brothers ranged as far north as Montana.

"There's one more thing," he said. "She's not to know anybody was asking about her."

"She won't hear it from me. She in trouble?"

"I don't know," Mayberly said.

5

THE TWO men and the boy followed a weaving course over the uneven land, avoiding the roads and the settlements, seeking the cover of canyons and timber. Most of the time they rode in file with the boy in the middle. When they were in country where they were apt to meet somebody, Tucker Ambrose rode on ahead as if he were not with the other two. The law would be looking for two men and a boy. One man and a boy were not likely to arouse anyone's suspicion.

Stevie felt better today. Thanks to Uncle Tucker's application of bacon grease and tobacco juice, the saddle sores were healing. The welts that Pa had put on him with an inch-thick willow stick were better too. They no longer brought searing, nauseating pain with every movement of the horse. And his appetite had come back. Before they set out this morning, he had eaten three of Uncle Tucker's flapjacks, each wrapped around a piece of bacon. It was the most he had eaten at one time since Pa had grabbed him that day behind the barn and taken him away from Aunt Melody.

He had made a mistake at the very beginning, he guessed. He had tried to hit Pa with that hoe. Then when Pa had torn it away from him and clamped his hand over his mouth, he had bitten Pa's hand. When they met Uncle Tucker, waiting at Five-Mile Creek with the extra horse, Pa had made a joke about his sore hand. They had ridden all that night and Pa had kept on making jokes about it. By morning Stevie understood that there was a bitterness behind the jokes. Down deep, Pa was pretty mad about being bitten.

The smart thing would have been to pretend to be glad to see Pa and willing to go with him. Then maybe they wouldn't have watched him so close and tied him up at night. Maybe Pa wouldn't have given him that beating three nights ago.

Uncle Tucker had tied him and he hadn't done a good job of it. Stevie had been able to work his hand loose and be a lot more comfortable. Later, he had to get up. Instead of calling out and waking Pa, as he was supposed to, he untied his feet and stole quietly off into the bush. When he had relieved himself, he went on a few yards to the edge of a bluff to look down on a dark valley with a river stretching through it like a silver ribbon. He supposed there were people down there. He thought of making a run for it and decided against it. Even if he found a way to get down there and got to a farm, Pa and Uncle Tucker would find him. They would kill the people at the farm, likely as not.

All of a sudden Pa had come up behind him. He grabbed Stevie by the hair and led him back to camp. He made him strip naked and cut the willow stick and laid it on. Uncle Tucker watched for a dozen licks and then said quietly that that was enough.

"He knew he was supposed to wake me up," Pa said, his voice shrill with anger and excitement. "He's damn well going to learn to do what I say and do it exact. He ain't never had proper respect for me, not

41

since he bit me. He's going to get it now. And he's going to learn what 'exact' means."

The stick sang through the air again and slashed Stevie's thighs. Stevie had tried from the beginning not to yell, but after the first few blows he lost control of himself. It was as if the yells and the sobs came from a part of him that he hadn't known was there.

"He won't be able to ride tomorrow," Uncle Tucker said.

"Exact is exact!" Pa said. The stick cut again.

"Sip" Uncle Tucker's voice was crisp now. "I'm puttin' my foot down."

It was usually Pa who used that expression. When they disagreed about something and their tempers were beginning to rise, he would say, "I'm puttin' my foot down," and that would be the end of it. Uncle Tucker would shut up and Pa would have his way. Now Uncle Tucker had said it and, surprisingly, it seemed to work both ways. Pa stopped the whipping. He tossed the stick across the ashes of the dead fire.

Uncle Tucker had built up the fire. He had poured half a sack of tobacco into a tomato can with a little water and boiled it. He had melted bacon grease, left over from supper, in the frying pan. He applied the tobacco juice to Stevie's wounds as he had done before to the saddle sores. Then he had applied the bacon grease.

Pa had sat and talked for a long time, his eyes glassy in the firelight. His voice was soft and gentle now, but the words were not.

"We're outlaws, son. You know that. Little men make laws and hide behind them. Well, Tuck and me, we ain't little men. We ain't going to abide by laws made up to work against us. We done pretty well. We got all the money we need. But the little men is after us. All the time. They even put a bounty on us. Besides the lawmen, we got bounty hunters after us and Pinkerton men, too, hired by the Colorado Bankers Association. So we got to live a special way, a hard way. We ain't bloodthirsty, but if a man is a danger to us, we kill him. That's the way it is when you're an outlaw. Sometimes it's him or you.

"Now we found us a place where we're going to live till folks ain't after us so hard. It ain't a bad place and if we're careful we'll be safe. But we got to be careful all the time. Extra careful. We can't count on nobody but ourselves. So when one of us says he'll do something, he does it. He does it exact. If he don't, we could all get killed. You ought to think about that."

Stevie was lying on his stomach. He was lying close to the fire, but he was shivering. Uncle Tucker came over and laid another blanket over him.

"There's something else you ought to think hard about," Pa said. "You ain't going back to your Aunt Melody. Not never. I made up my mind to that and you got to make up your mind to it. If you try to go back to her, I will find her and kill her. You can't go back to her if she's dead, now can you?"

Stevie had lain awake the rest of the night, too sore to breathe, almost, and quaking with intermittent chills. He kept thinking of Aunt Melody and sometimes he sobbed softly.

That had been three nights ago, and the next two days had been a pure hell of soreness. But he was better now. He would remember that word "exact" and

43

apply it to everything Pa ordered him to do. As long as Pa didn't beat him too often, he could stand the rest of it. It might be a long time before he got his chance, years maybe. But sometime, somewhere, he was going to find a way to get back to Aunt Melody.

He had no idea where they were now except that it was Wyoming. They had traveled west mostly but today they had turned north. He gathered that there was a special place Pa hoped to get to before night, a camp where they would get fresh horses or something.

Late in the afternoon they passed close to a town. Uncle Tucker rode ahead, and Pa and Stevie followed a mile or so behind. At one point they rode along the edge of a fenced hayfield with a farmhouse a stone's throw away, and a man came into the yard and hailed them. Pa waved at him and kept going straight ahead at a steady pace. The man called out and came running toward them. Pa cussed and swung to meet him.

"Keep you mouth shut," he said to Stevie.

The man was out of breath. His shirttail was out in back. He was wild-eyed with excitement.

"Mister, I need help. My wife has come down with something bad. Stomach cramps and puking and a hell of a fever. I'm afraid it's typhoid. I'm scared to leave and go for the doctor. Would you do it for me?"

"Where's he at?"

"Sheridan."

"We just come from there," Pa said. "I'll tell you what I'll do. I'll ride on to your next neighbor and give him the word."

"Nearest neighbor north is a drunken old hermit who don't own a horse. If you was to turn back and take the road south, the McLaughlin place

44

ain't more'n a mile and a half. I reckon one of them would ride to town, all right."

Pa nodded agreeably. "I got to meet a man north of here first. If I don't get a move on, I'll miss him. But don't you worry none. After I meet him, I'll ride back and send one of those folks for the doctor."

"Mister, this is life or death. Could you send the boy? He could ride down to McLaughlin's and catch up to you later."

"The boy don't know this country and he would get lost," Pa said irritably. "You go back to your wife and don't worry. The doctor will be along. I'll see to it."

The man looked like he was going to cuss Pa good. Instead, he swallowed hard and let out kind of a sob.

"All right, mister. But hurry. Please. Jesus, mister, this is life or death."

"Don't worry none," Pa said. "Come on, boy."

A couple of miles farther along they came on Uncle Tucker. He was sitting on the ground in the shade of a little clump of poplars, letting his horse graze. Pa and Stevie got down from their horses, too, and Pa and Uncle Tucker talked for awhile. They talked about the route ahead and how much farther it was to the place they were headed for.

Pa seemed to have forgotten about the sick woman. Stevie reminded him of it. Pa had to explain what had happened, and this irritated him. It was plain now that he had *wanted* to forget.

"You said you'd get word to a doctor?" Uncle Tucker asked.

"Course I did. What else could I do?"

"We better do it then, Sip. I'll do it."

"You forget about it. The goddamn woman has probably got the summer complaint and the fool clodhopper thinks it's typhoid."

"Suppose she's really sick and the doctor don't come. That man won't forget your meanness. He'll wonder why you was in such a hell of a hurry. He'll remember you had a boy with you. He'll talk about it. There's a telegraph in Sheridan. They'll have heard about you taking the boy. Sooner or later—"

"That's foolishness," Pa said. "After tomorrow, it won't make a particle of difference."

"It still wouldn't hurt to do it."

"That man already has had a good look at me and the boy," Pa said. "No sense in giving some other folks a good look at us. No, Tuck. I'm puttin' my foot down."

"Sip, you said yourself—"

"*I'm puttin' my foot down on it.*"

Uncle Tucker shrugged and that was the end of it.

In a little while they had climbed into wild lonesome country where many of the slopes were covered with pine. The sun touched a ragged black line of mountains and slid behind them. Dust in the air caught the afterglow and the world was bathed by amber light. When Pa and Uncle Tucker decided they were close to their destination, Uncle Tucker went ahead to scout.

Pa and Stevie rode into a stand of pine and got off their horses to wait. Stevie lay prone on the soft duff and rested his head on his arms. Pa sat down with his back against a tree.

"I reckon you're still thinkin' of that sick woman," Pa said.

"Some," Stevie admitted.

46

"Like I told you, son, the little people of this world is against us. They got their ways, which has nothing to do with us. We don't owe them nothing. You understand that?"

"What if that woman dies?"

"She ain't likely to die, but it don't matter if she does. It don't matter a-tall."

Pa's jaw was set hard. A hint of shrillness had crept into his voice. He had that same glary-eyed look he'd had when he swung the willow stick. Stevie was suddenly scared.

"I reckon I'll learn," he said quickly.

Pa eyed him sharply and then chuckled. "You dang right you'll learn. And don't you ever try to deceive me. You do, I'll give you a *real* hiding. What I give you the other night ain't nothing to what you'll get if you try to deceive me."

Stevie forced himself to grin. "I'm not used to being an outlaw, that's all. I got a whole lot to learn, and it isn't easy to learn all at once."

Pa grunted and seemed satisfied with that. He leaned his head back against the tree and closed his eyes.

It was dusk when Uncle Tucker got back and they mounted up. The sky was a thickening gray with streaks of lavender in it. They turned up a creek into heavy timber. In a little while they came suddenly to a cabin with a small fenced pasture adjoining it. There was a team of harness horses in the pasture. A farm wagon that had been rigged with a canvas cover was parked near the cabin door.

They got down from their horses and a man came out of the cabin and shook hands with Pa. He was a small man, not much bigger than Uncle Tucker, and he had a full beard. They unsaddled the horses, turned them into the pasture, and went into the cabin. A pot of coffee and a pan of stew were cooking on the small stove. The man spooned stew into tin plates and set them on the rickety table. They sat down on log blocks that had been sawed to the right size for stools. The stew was hot and fragrant and there were dumplings in it. Stevie ate greedily.

The bearded man had a tense, worried way about him. Pa and Uncle Tucker called him "Fletch," and he looked startled every time they did it. After a while Stevie decided that that was a name he didn't go by any more.

"I ought to start home right away," Fletch said. "It would look better if I didn't stay away all night."

"No objections," Pa said. "How much do we owe you?"

"The team cost a hundred and fifty dollars. You said to get a good one, and this is the best I could find without going into fancy stock. Wagon cost ninety. You said you didn't want a new-looking cover on it, so I used an old tarp I had. I'll charge you a dollar for it. Clothes and supplies ran about fifteen dollars. Whole thing totals out at two hundred and fifty-five dollars and forty-five cents."

"Add something on for yourself."

"I owe you a favor or two, Sip. I'm glad to do it."

Pa grinned one-sidedly. "Fact is you're scared not to do it."

"Some truth in that," Fletch admitted.

Pa produced an oilskin wallet and counted out four hundred dollars in fifty-dollar bills.

"That gives you almost a hundred and fifty dollars for your trouble," he said. "You can have our saddle horses to boot. They're all fifty-dollar animals. They're wore down some but they ain't lame and they'll fatten up nice."

"I sure appreciate this," Fletch said, picking up the money. "I don't pretend I can't use it."

"You should've stayed with me and Tuck for a couple more jobs."

"Well, I had my share of the take from that stage and express office. It seemed like all the money in the world. I got married and bought the farm and it was gone. I even got a debt on the place now."

Pa pushed away his plate and tilted back on the chunk of log he was sitting on. "If we was to be taken, we would name you as the third man on the express job, Fletch. You understand that. The man who done the shooting."

Fletch laughed uneasily. "I understand, Sip. I got a real interest in seeing you stay free."

Fletch left a few minutes later, taking the saddle horses. After he had gone, Pa stood in the doorway and stared into the night for a time. Uncle Tucker was stretched out on one of the two bunks that made a right angle in a corner of the cabin. Stevie had spread his blankets on the floor and was lying on his stomach, half-asleep. The lantern on the table steadied and brightened as Pa closed the door.

"What's he so nervous about?" Pa said.

"He don't like to be reminded about that stage office," Uncle Tucker said. "He's a honest farmer now."

"Honest!" Pa said. He sank down on the other

bunk. "There ain't but one honest critter on this earth and that's a pack rat. When he makes off with something, he leaves something for it, something he considers to be valuable. He has honesty built into him by nature. But a man don't. He don't have nothing built into him but twisticalness."

"Some men are scared," Uncle Tucker said. "They're scared of what folks think of 'em or of the law or of God. Being scared makes 'em honest."

"That's foolishness. Being scared is just as likely to make 'em dishonest."

"Not if they're scared of God."

"There ain't no God," Pa said.

That shocked Stevie. He had wondered about God sometimes, but he had never doubted Him, Pa was eying him.

"You believe in God, boy?"

"Yes, sir."

"Well, get over it. It's a lie."

Pa began to pull off his boots. Stevie turned over on his back. He stared up at the pattern of the log rafters, shadow-swept in the lantern light. There were cobwebs up there, which were made by spiders. Where did spiders come from if God didn't make them? It was a terrifying question.

Pa took off his gunbelt. He drew the big revolver from its holster and dropped the belt on top of his boots. He laid the gun on the far side of the bunk and stretched out.

"I ain't going to tie you tonight," he said. "I'll hear you if you move around, though. Blow out that lantern."

Stevie got up, feeling scared and empty and not

wanting to be in the dark just yet. He turned down the lantern flame, levered up the chimney, and blew. The saffron flame danced before his eyes as he stumbled back to his blankets.

"I don't know," Uncle Tucker said drowsily. "Seems like there might be a God. Maybe He ain't like the preachers say He is. I hope He ain't. But it seems like there might be one."

That took away some of the frightening empty feeling. The dancing lantern flame faded and went away. The cabin was drowsy-warm and a comfortable change from sleeping on the ground, even though the floor was kind of hard. It was nice not to be tied, too, and Stevie fell asleep quickly.

He woke in a convulsion of crashing explosions and stabbing flame. Something thudded to the floor near the door. Then there was utter silence and the sick-sweet smell of gunpowder, the itchy feeling of dust sifting down from the rafters. Pa's voice was far away.

"Lay still."

Stevie realized he had been deafened by the gunshots inside the small building. Pa appeared in a sudden shifting island of light, touching a match to the lantern. The door was open and a draft tore at the flame. Pa lifted the lantern and moved toward the door. A man lay face down just inside the cabin. Pa probed him with a stockinged foot, then squatted and rolled him over.

Uncle Tucker was sitting on the edge of his bunk, revolver in hand. "Fletch?"

"Yep," Pa said. "The damn fool."

"Dead?"

"Dead."

Pa picked up something from beside the body and held it up. It was a hatchet.

"Meant to kill us in our beds," Pa said.

Stevie got to his feet, gaping, unable to take his eyes off the body.

"He was hurting for that reward money," Pa said. "I had a hunch. I was laying awake."

"He couldn't turn us in alive because of that express company job," Uncle Tucker agreed. "He had to do it dead."

"He would've had to do for the boy too," Pa said indignantly. "You see how it is, boy? We got to watch our p's and q's all the time or we'll be dead. All of us."

"Well, we got a problem now," Uncle Tucker said. "Fletch had a wife. He claimed she didn't know where he was or what he was up to. I reckon that's probably true. But she'll miss him and folks will come looking for him."

"Nothing to do but bury him back in the woods someplace," Pa said.

They did it right then, carrying the body between them while Stevie carried the lantern and an old rusty shovel. They scooped out a grave in the duff, next to a fallen tree, and dumped the body into it.

In the morning they went back and rolled the fallen tree over the grave. Then they raked the duff around so the place looked natural and undisturbed. Back at the cabin, they cleaned up the blood. Uncle Tucker scouted around till he found the saddle horses. They would have to take the horses with them now, tied to the back of the wagon. Pa didn't like this much. The kind of folks they were going to pretend to be weren't likely to have three good riding horses, he said.

There was a suitcase in the wagon and it was packed with clothes. Pa put on a gray work shirt and a pair of overalls. Then he added a rumpled black suit coat and a low-crowned, broad-brimmed black hat. He looked like a Quaker farmer, sort of.

Uncle Tucker stripped down to his underwear and tied a kind of sash around his chest. He stuffed a towel into the front of it. Then he got into a loose-fitting calico dress. He put on black stockings and women's shoes. When he had draped a shawl over his shoulders and tied on a poke bonnet, he truly looked like a little dark-eyed woman. He was pretty, almost.

"You got any laughing to do, you do it right now," he said to Stevie. "There ain't going to be no laughing once we get in that wagon."

"From now on you call him 'Ma,'" Pa said. "That ain't a joke. You do it. You slip just once when folks is around and we're dead."

They hitched the team to the wagon and started out. The saddle horses were strung out behind, the first tied to the wagon with a lead rope and the next tied to his tail and the third tied to the tail of the second. In a little while they reached a road and took it, headed north. They crossed the Montana line that afternoon and camped along a creek, where they caught some trout for supper.

The next day it rained, but they kept moving, thankful for the covered wagon. Travel was easy now, compared to horseback. They took turns driving, and there was plenty of time for sleeping. Pa seemed to feel good and he did a lot of singing. Stevie knew some of the songs and joined in and Pa seemed pleased.

They headed northwest, moving slowly out of the grassy, rolling, plateau country toward the spine of the Rockies. Stevie lost track of the days. After about a week, they came to a town called Spinnerville. They bought supplies here and then camped in a grove of alders on a riverbank half a mile out of town. The campsite was hidden from town by a low ridge. It was off the road and no one came near them and they stayed there two days.
~~stayed there two days.~~

On the afternoon of the second day a young woman walked into camp from the direction of town. Pa and Uncle Tucker had been expecting her and Pa kissed her. She didn't recognize Uncle Tucker at first and was amazed to find that that was him in the woman's clothes. She kissed him, too, then. She said she was so tired from traveling that she was ready to drop, and the first thing she did was take off her clothes and take a bath in the river, right in front of everybody.

That night when they had finished supper and were sitting around the fire, Pa did a lot of serious talking.

"We're going to a place north of here," he said. "It's not more'n a couple of hours by wagon. It's called New Sanity—maybe you heard of it. The folks there is what you would call peculiar. They is full of peculiar ideas, of which I don't understand 'em all. The important thing is they keep to themselves and strangers don't come around much. I was there a while back, wearin' these same clothes. I made arrangements for us to join 'em and live in New Sanity.

"This is the last place anybody would go lookin' for the Ambrose brothers. Just the same, if two men and a boy was to show up there, somebody might get his suspicions up. So we are going there as a family. Tucker has passed as a woman before. He is good at it and nobody has ever suspected. There is just one thing. He can say 'Yes' or 'No' or 'I guess so' in a soft woman's voice just fine. He is not so good if he has to put a whole lot of words together. So if somebody gets to asking him complicated questions, one of us has got to cut in and get their attention.

"My name is Edward Johnson. Tucker is my wife, Helen Johnson. The boy is Robert Johnson and we call him Bob. Susanna is Tucker's sister. I don't see no reason for her to change her name. We'll call her Sue. Now you all practice those names. Get them straight and on the tip of your tongue. Boy, what's your name?"

"Bob," Stevie said.

"Bob what?"

"Johnson."

Susanna was sitting next to Stevie. She slipped her arm around him and smiled down at him.

"From now on I'm your Aunt Sue," she said. "Do you think you'll like that?"

She wrapped her hair in a towel. Her eyes were big and black and her teeth were white and even. She smelled soapy and kind of sweet. She was nice, he guessed, but he felt a sharp aching longing for Aunt Melody. He looked into the fire and replied dutifully.

"Yes, ma'am."

"We leave early in the morning," Pa said.

6

MABERLY SPENT more than an hour poking around the campsite. Near as he could tell, it had been abandoned about two days. There had been no rain in that time and there were plenty of footprints and other sign. The trick was to make it add up to something.

He had trailed Susanna Velasquez on her stage ride across Wyoming, trading his horse for a fresh one four times. He had been satisfied to stay well behind her and had reached Spinnerville a day after she did. He had found several people, including the sheriff, who had seen her get off the stage, take her carpetbag from the driver, and turn down the street in the direction of the hotel. But no lone woman had checked in that day. There were two rooming houses in town, but he found that she had gone to neither of them. For a time, it seemed as if she had vanished like a puff of smoke.

After a day and a half of inquiring, he had got a lead from the town barber, who had watched the arrival of the stage that day from his shop window. She had walked past the hotel and right out of town, the barber said. The Methodist church and parsonage were off by themselves, a hundred yards from the last buildings; he assumed she had gone there.

Mayberly had called on the minister and learned she had not. However, the minister, who liked to fish, reported that a party had been camped on the river a little way downstream. The place was well off the road, but he supposed it was possible she joined the people there.

Mayberly was reasonably sure now that she had. The dainty footprint with the small heel and pointed toe seemed to confirm it. It was made by a shoe a woman dressed for stagecoach travel might wear. Fashionable rather than practical. Not a walking shoe. It seemed logical that she might have joined the Ambrose brothers here. But when Mayberly sorted out the other prints, he was not at all sure of that.

There was the man's bootprint. That was plain enough. And there was the print of a child's shoe—the boy's probably. Finally, and this was the confusing thing, there was the mark of another woman's shoe. Then there were the hoofmarks. It seemed as if a man, a woman, and a boy had been traveling in a wagon drawn by a pair of good-sized harness horses. And three lighter horses had been with the party. Well, such an outfit should be easy enough to trace, he thought.

He went back to the road. It was plain from the angle at which the wagon had entered that it had turned north—toward town. Later traffic had, of course, pulverized any sign it had left in the road.

He walked back to Spinnerville edgy and dissatisfied. He had a feeling he had missed something that should have been obvious. And there was the annoying possibility that the footprint he took to be Susanna's was not hers at all. Or she could have met a party that had nothing to do with the Ambrose brothers at all. There were a number of other possibilities. The little that he had learned was only enough to tinder almost endless speculation.

Spinnerville was the county seat, so there were several lawyers' offices tucked in among the other businesses in the score of buildings along the main street. The courthouse, the only stone building in town, was at the north end of town. It was set back a little way from the street and had a well-kept lawn and a flagpole in front of it. Mayberly cut across the lawn and found his way to the sheriff's office on the second floor of the long, stale-smelling building.

The sheriff was a middle-aged man with a gaunt face and curly gray hair. He was wearing steel-rimmed spectacles and was busy with paper work. He looked over the spectacles at Mayberly.

"You again? Find your woman?"

"You know anything about some folks camped on the river half a mile south?" Mayberly asked.

"Noticed 'em. They were in town a few days back. Bought a few things. Man and a woman and a boy. They got something to do with the gal you're looking for?"

"Looks like she joined 'em."

"They've moved on?"

"Couple of days ago, I'd say. How old was the boy?"

"I don't know. Nine or ten."

"You talk to any of 'em?"

"I didn't even give 'em a second look. Nothing suspicious about 'em. You ask a hell of a lot of questions. If you didn't have that letter from H. B. Tovey, I'd throw you out."

Mayberly grinned. "What did they look like?"

"Farmers on the move. Going visiting maybe or off to take up a homestead someplace. Or maybe horse traders. They were leading three fair-looking horses. Suppose you tell me just exactly what you're looking for, Mr. Mayberly. If I knew that I might be of more help. Seems like it might be country business anyway."

The sheriff took off his glasses and laid them on top of the papers on his desk. His hostility was tempered by friendly eyes and a half-serious tone of voice. He looked tough and intelligent. Mayberly decided that he liked him.

"What's north of here, Sheriff?"

"Next town on the stage road is Star City. Old boom town with only an echo left. It's darn near thirty miles straight north. Fifteen miles farther along the road hits the N.P. tracks. No town there. The road follows the tracks west to Three Forks."

"There's nothing between here and Star City?"

"Couple of way stations. There's the colony, of course, but that's east. Red Horse Road joins the stage road just north of town and leads straight to it."

"You lost me there," Mayberly said. "The colony?"

'Place called New Sanity. Some folks around here call it Insanity."

"I've heard the name. Didn't realize it was so close. A bunch of Shaking Quakers or something like that, isn't it?"

"Fifteen years ago it was a Shaker colony, and about to die out. It's said those Shakers were so pure they didn't produce offspring, which is more or less true. But it was poverty that was about to wipe 'em out, not purity. The trouble was high land with a short growing season and uncertain rainfall. Their crops dried up year after year. Then this Dr. Favra showed up and took over. Jacob Boehme Favra. Calls himself a Fourierist, which seems to be sort of the opposite of a Shaker, far as purity goes. A lot of the Shakers were offended by his ideas and moved out.

59

Maybe half of them stayed, though. They still follow their old ways up in the north end of the valley. A different sort came along and took over the south part. A lot of 'em are well educated people. Freethinkers and such. They share everything, the talk is, including their wives.

"Well, this Favra has held 'em all together, Shakers and freethinkers and whatnot. He built a dam on a little stream called Singing River and got the farms on their feet. They raise pretty good wheat up there now and enough truck and livestock to feed themselves. They aren't rich, but nobody's starving.

"There was considerable opposition to the dam by the rest of the county. This is cattle country and Favra has bought up several sections of range land from the Northern Pacific and converted it to wheat. Feeling still runs high. But there are more than three hundred adult males up there in New Sanity. They had never had any interest in wordly things like politics. Well, Favra had them all register to vote. They don't vote; they just keep themselves on the registration list. Since there are only about eight hundred votes in the whole county, including New Sanity, Favra holds the balance of power. He could swing any election any time he wants to, just by telling his people to vote.

"So we are damn nice to those people up there. They pay their taxes and we leave 'em alone, which is what their want. They govern themselves, enforce their own laws. I stay away. Mostly, they leave us alone too; but when Favra talks, we listen. And when he wants to build a dam, he builds it."

"Doesn't sound like a place a man on the run would head for," Mayberly said.

"Thought you were looking for a woman," the sheriff

said.

"Both."

"They wanted by the law?"

"Not the woman, far as I know."

"I take it the man is. That makes it my business, Mr. Mayberly. Who is he?"

"You agree to lay off, leave him to me?"

"If he's in my county, I don't agree to one damn thing."

Maberly had taken a chair to one side of the desk and had tilted back in it. Now the front legs thumped the floor and he got to his feet.

"I'm tailing the Ambrose brothers, Sheriff. At least I hope I am. I've got a hunch that the woman who got off that stage came up here to join 'em. Just a hunch. Sip Ambrose took his son from a farm in South Dakota a few weeks ago. You must have heard about it. That could be the boy with the folks in the wagon, although none of it fits together as well as I'd like. I could be dead wrong about the whole business, but I'm riding north now to try to find that wagon. If I don't, I'll be back. In the meantime, I assume you're too sensible to spread talk about this. That would bring a crop of professional man hunters down on you and it would have half your local people ready to shoot any stranger who rides through here."

The sheriff listened closely, his eyes narrow in a network of fine little wrinkles. "If you spot 'em in my county, Mayberly, I want to know it."

"I'll agree to that if you'll agree to leave the planning to me."

"I take it you're interested in the reward."

"You're damn right I am. I've been studying the Ambrose boys a long time. I'm the man who is going to take 'em and the reward is mine, all of it. You can have the glory and the votes it will buy.''

The sheriff got to his feet, impatience twitching in his face. "There's such a thing as a man finding pride in doing the job he's paid for, Mayberly. I'll say that once. You make me want to mention it again and I'll run you clean out of Montana.''

Mayberly laughed. "Maybe we're beginning to understand each other. One more favor, Sheriff. I wrote a letter to a woman in Colorado, telling her to join me here. She'll be using the name of Russell. Her real name is Melody Coates. She's Sip Ambrose's sister-in-law, the boy's aunt. If I can't meet her here, she'll wait till she hears from me. I tell you this so you won't go bothering her with a lot of questions.''

The sheriff's nod was almost imperceptible. He came around the desk, gave Mayberly his hand, and wished him good luck.

For a few minutes he watched from the county assessor's office at the front of the building until he saw Mayberly ride north out of town. He got his hat then and went to the livery barn, where the county kept half a dozen good horses and a buggy. He hitched up the buggy and he, too, traveled north. But at the first crossroads he turned east toward New Sanity.

7

JACOB BOEHME FAVRA paced the huge room that served as headquarters for the New Sanity community. The room took up almost half of the second floor of the hundred-foot-long brick building known as the phalanstery. It was a well-lighted, rather barren room. It was furnished with three desks, several simple pine chairs, and a few small braided rugs laid in a neat row down the center. One of the desks was a roll top and was tucked into a corner near one of the large, uncurtained, multiple-light windows. The other two desks were flat tops and faced each other across the row of rugs. The colony's vice-president, Elwood Snowe, sat at one of them buisly scribbling figures.

Favra sighed noisily. "The sheriff has cooled his heels long enough. Go down and tell him I'll see him now."

Elwood Snowe got to his feet. He was a small, bald man with a fringe of dark hair and long, grey-flecked sideburns. He shuffled a sheaf of papers and shoved them into a drawer. He had a nervous quickness about him that irritated Favra.

"Don't answer any questions," Favra said. "Now or later. And, Elwood. I'd better see the man alone."

"Certainly. As a matter of fact, I was about to ride out to the dam."

"What for?"

"I want to inspect the needle gates. They're new, you

know. We tried a new process to make the wood water-resistant.''

"Of course, I know.'' Favra smiled quickly to cover his annoyance. "By all means, Elwood, have a look at them.''

Snowe left the room, perking with purpose. A steaming little coffeepot of a man, Favra thought. He had taken over the details of administration energetically and efficiently. That was a great help. But he had also developed a proprietary attitude. Especially toward the dam. And the dam was Favra's. He had conceived it, helped design it, overseen its building. It had saved New Sanity from poverty and dissolution and he looked upon it as a monument of his leadership.

The river began as a small wild thing in the high country. Fed to a flashing torrent by creeks and watershed, it ricocheted off Bluestone Mountain and screamed northward through a steep-walled canyon. Then it squeezed out into the broad thirty-mile-long valley where the colony's farms lay. Favra had at once seen the opportunity for a reservoir in the long deep canyon. This foresight had established his position in the colony and had brought him a feeling of success for the first time in the many long years since he had graduated from Harvard.

Immediately after graduation, he had married a bookish English girl and had set out for his first parish full of confidence. But his ideas, to which he was firmly dedicated, were far too liberal for the times, even for Unitarians. There came a Sunday when he entered the pulpit to find himself with a congregation of one—his wife. Doggedly, he had preached his sermon. Afterward, he had gone home and got drunk.

After that he had shuttled from one indigent backcountry parish to another. He tried to tone down his preaching and found that eloquence and conviction left him. Finally, he left the church entirely and began to seek out groups of freethinkers. He was better received now, but his audiences were made up mostly of misfits as poor as himself. The collection plate seldom held a coin larger than a dime.

Frugality and frustration wore his wife into a lingering illness. At thirty-six, he found himself a widower. A few years later he was involved in a scandal with a girl of sixteen. Penniless, disgraced, facing tar and feathers, he had done the only sensible thing left. He had gone west.

On the way, he stopped over at New Harmony, Indiana, where his lectures got a warm reception and earned him several weeks of hospitality. After that he visited other communistic colonies and found that even the strictly religious ones were good for a few nights' bed and board. At New Sanity (called Serenity then) he had confined his remarks to matters of economics, having learned that Shakers were not offended by liberalism in this area. He was treated cordially and he stayed on. When he broached the idea of a dam, the enthusiasm of the desperate people amazed him. He found himself appointed a member of the governing body and in charge of the project.

He knew nothing of dams, but it seemed to him that one could be built with local labor and little capital. Recklessly, he had said the job could be done in a year. By great luck he found a former Swiss schoolteacher living near the colony, a mathematician who had a least a vague idea of the principles of dam building. Together, they had worked out stresses and pressures, determined weights and inclinations, and designed a simple earth-fill dam with masonry faces and a brick core wall. The health of the Swiss was so poor (he died a few years later) that he was of little use on the job. Favra had taken over the chore of supervision and had found himself competent at it. He had seen the work completed in a year to the day.

As if to make up for all the wasted years, Fate threw him still another kiss. The dam proved to be the boon he had predicted. By the second year he had seen to the construction of a network of irrigation ditches and had learned a good deal about water storage and the regulation of flow. Land that had been worthless for anything but grazing began to bloom.

Favra got the credit. When the colony's president died, he was an almost unanimous choice to take over the office.

He had never been sympathetic to Shakerism with its emphasis on celibacy, physically exhausting worship, spirit messages. He brought in friends from other colonies. He maneuvered some of them onto the council. When he had control of it, he proclaimed a "doctrine of non-doctrine." Members were to be free to follow any religious bent they chose. Or none at all. The Fourieristic custom of sharing women was to be permitted among those who saw no harm in it.

The angry turmoil that followed was brief. Many of the Shakers left. Their places were promptly taken by new members sympathetic to Favra's views. Most of these came from other communistic societies that had sprung up in America in the early part of the century and now were breaking up or reverting to capitalist economics.

The Shakers who remained in the north half of the valley continued in their old ways. Each group held its own meetings several times a week. Once a week there was a general meeting in a converted barn on the east side of the valley. They were represented on the council. They were as well fed and clothed as the Fourierists in the south part of the valley. They continued to be outraged by the wife sharing that the Fourierists practiced. But by and large, the Shakers made no trouble. They were too devoted to their own mystical welfare to spend much time trying to reform this world.

As for the Fourierists, Favra considered that they basked in the intellectual good life. No one was required to work more than thirty hours a week. Social life centered around literary societies, debating clubs, discussion groups. There were concerts, readings, plays. All children attended school. Favra's goal now was a full "phalanx," a colony of 1620 people. This was the number that Fourier had considered ideal. He had been quietly buying up land. He had, in fact, gone a bit too fast. The colony's cash reserve was used up. . . .

The sheriff's knock was brisk and business-like. Favra waited until it was repeated before he opened the door.

"I won't take up much of your time," the sheriff said. "I'm after a bit of information and it seemed best to come straight to you."

"Of course. Find a chair."

The sheriff did not sit down. He was a shade taller than Favra, and Favra resented that. He strode behind one of the two facing desks and raised himself to his toes. By touching the desk with the fingertips of one hand, he could hold this position of several minutes without teetering.

"I'd like to know if you have some newcomers here," the sheriff said. "I don't know the name. There would be four of 'em. A man, two women, and a boy. They would have arrived by covered wagon day before yesterday."

"We've had several additions to the phalanx in the last

67

month. I don't recall the family you mention, but I could look in the records. We keep a running census, you know. What is your interest in these people?"

"Somebody is looking for 'em. I thought they might have come here."

"Somebody? Who?"

"Matter of fact, it's a bounty hunter."

Favra scowled his distaste. "They're wanted by the law?"

"It's more likely he believes they'll lead him to somebody who's wanted."

"And that person might be at New Sanity? Nonsense."

"I'd appreciate it if you'd look at that census."

Favra brushed past the sheriff and went around the other desk. He jerked open a drawer and extracted a dog-eared ledger. He leafed rapidly through it, ran a finger down a page.

"Byron J. Samuels and Dorothy Smith Samuels. No children. Arrived here the fourteenth. That's a week ago Saturday. They're our most recent members."

"Nobody since then?"

Favra snapped the book shut and dropped it on the desk with a slap. He rose to his toes again and regarded the sheriff with icy patience. He didn't bother to reply to a question he had already answered. His fingers tapped the desk.

After a pause, the sheriff said, "Guess I'm barking up the wrong tree."

"Sorry not to be of more help," Favra said. He took a step toward the door as if to show the sheriff out. "I trust you won't go around questioning our people about matters like this. We would deeply resent such an intrusion."

The sheriff's eyebrows went up. "In other words, you

might decide to vote."

"That's always a possibility, although we would prefer not to. We are not a worldly people."

"I leave you pretty much alone." The sheriff's eyes were small and hard. "That's worked fine. That's why I'm here right now. I thought you'd rather co-operate with me than have that bounty hunter nosing around."

"You're absolutely right. I'm sure we understand each other." Favra held out his hand. He produced a friendly, medium-warm smile.

The sheriff shook hands. He was not capable of a friendly, medium-warm smile and he didn't try. He said, "Then don't throw your weight on me, Dr. Favra, votes or no votes. When I have questions to ask, I'll come to you first. But any time that doesn't get satisfactory results, I'll question anybody in this county I damn well please."

He smiled very slightly now, nodded, and turned toward the door. Favra stood by the window to watch him ride away.

I lied, Favra thought. He didn't like to lie. Yet it was surely true that persons at the head of great enterprises had to rise above petty moral considerations. If there was an intelligent force behind the universe, it surely understood that. What bothered him was that the sheriff seemed to suspect that he was lying.

It was plain enough that the family in question was that of Ed Johnson. There was something peculiar about that bunch. Favra had realized that at once. But he would be the one to look into the matter, not the county sheriff.

Johnson had visited New Sanity two or three times in the last year. He had been alone each time. Favra seemed to remember a letter of introduction addressed to Elwood Snowe. He didin't remember ever having read it himself.

On the last visit, Johnson had applied for membership in the community. He said he had been convinced of the advantages of share-alike living in communities like this through the writings of Horace Greeley. Yet he was far from being an educated man and a skillful question or two had revealed his ignorance of the ideas of Greeley or any other writer on the subject. He wasn't the kind of man who would fit into the discussion groups or literary society. Moreover, he had asked for certain privileges. For one thing, he didn't want his son put into the compulsory school with the other children. Not at once, anyway. The boy was not well, he said. His aunt would teach him at home.

Johnson had also asked that a house be built for his family off to itself in the southeast corner of the valley on a site he had selected. He would bear the expense. In fact, he had laid a thousand eollars in cash on Favra's desk. That was more than enough for a modest building that would be quickly put up by colony carpenters.

If he had made the decision strictly on principle, Favra would have turned the man away. But Johnson obviously had money. The colony needed money much more desperately than it needed good Fourierists.

When a newcomer arrived, he was asked to turn his worldy wealth over to the colony. Most of those who joined were next to broke anyway. They were glad enough to give up their meager capital in return for the food, shelter, and clothing that would be supplied to them. The few who were well off had usually compromised by making a substantial gift and hanging on to the bulk of their property. There was really no hard and fast rule about the matter. Johnson had offered to put up five thousand dollars, and that had clinched his acceptance.

The money had come several weeks ago. It had come by express, a sealed package of fifty one-hundred-dollar bills addressed to Elwood Snowe.

The house was almost finished when the Johnsons arrived. Johnson had said he would do the remaining work himself. He made it clear that he and his family would keep to themselves. At Favra's insistence, he had allowed himself to be introduced at a council meeting the first night he was here, but that was about all anyone had seen of him. He had come to the meeting with his sister-in-law, explaining that Mrs. Johnson was indisposed from the trip. He had been courteous and friendly but a little stand-offish too. The sister-in-law had been charming, particularly to Favra. He had found himself talking to her at greath length about the colony and himself. He had especially enjoyed explaining Fourieristic sex practices to her. She seemed never to have heard of them, but she was not at all shocked. She had fixed her big black eyes on him and had seemed fascinated.

No, it wouldn't do for the sheriff or that bounty hunter he had mentioned to come around asking questions about the Johnsons. Favra would do his own investigating in his own way. He was sure Elwood Snowe knew more about them than he was letting on. If they were actually wanted by the law or involved with outlaws—well, he would assume for the time being that they weren't. In the meantime, he would see that nothing happened to make other members of the colony suspicious of them. Especially members of the Patrol.

He didn't much care for the Patrol, but it was a necessity. He had formed it years ago when a number of cowboys had begun to hang around New Sanity. They were under the impression that the women of the colony were available to anyone who made the effort. When told that they were not welcome, they had responded with arrogance and belligerence. Some of the unmarried girls had made things worse by teasing them a bit. The Patrol had dealt with the intruders swiftly and decisively. Favra knew no details and wanted to know none.

Since that time, the dozen stern members of the Patrol had done what little other police work there was to do. Yes, the Patrol was a regrettable necessity. At the same time, it was comforting to know that it was there. If that bounty hunter should show up, for instance, the Patrol would handle him once and for all.

8

UNCLE TUCKER was drunk.

They had hidden his guns and his throwing knife and were watching him every second. He wore his woman's clothing but he was not acting like a woman except to clown around. He was not wearing the poke bonnet. Aunt Sue had let them cut off some of her hair and had made him a switch that was almost the right color. It was pinned to this head but his own hair was sticking out around it and he looked ridiculous. Sometimes he was very funny. He made them all laugh, even Pa, when he pretended to see a mouse and jumped on top of the table and threw his skirt over his head. Stevie laughed until his sides hurt.

Twice, Uncle Tucker ran out of the house and tried to catch a horse, for gosh knew what reason. Pa went after him and brought him back inside. The second time, Pa hit him and knocked him down. He picked him up and would have hit him again, but Aunt Sue ran out and grabbed Pa's arm. He slapped Aunt Sue then and she stood there and dared him to do it again.

"Go ahead," she said. "Black my eyes. How will we explain that to Dr. Favra?"

Pa did not hit her again. He led Uncle Tucker into the house and set him down at the table. He poured a water glass full of whisky and set it in front of him.

Uncle Tucker stared at it a while, sipped it, and then drank it in about two gulps. He started to sing, then and got up and grabbed Aunt Sue and started to dance. Pa went over to the table and filled up the glass again.

"Only thing to do is get him exflunctified," Pa said.

Aunt Sue spoke over Tucker's shoulder. "What if this happened when you and I were at that council meeting and he was alone with Stevie?"

"It wouldn't happen at a time like that," Pa said. "Not unless he'd already started. He don't start drinking unless I'm there to look after him."

"Horsefeathers," Aunt Sue said.

"Aunt Sue was a puzzle to Stevie. She was real nice to him. When Pa got mad at him, she stepped in and smoothed thing over. But when he got mad at her, she said things that just made him madder. Sometimes she got slapped or got her arm twisted. Or both. Stevie didn't understand why she stood for that. It seemed like she could tell Pa to keep his hands off her or she would up and leave. But she never did. It was as if she *liked* being hurt, almost.

At other times, it was like she was in love with Pa. They would do a lot of hugging and kissing. But then she did that with Uncle Tucker too. Stevie guessed she was what Aunt Melody would call a loose woman. He wasn't sure he knew exactly what that meant, but he latched onto the term as an explanation of all the things he didn't understand about Aunt Sue.

The main part of the house was without partitions; it was kitchen, dining room, and parlor all together. Pa had walked to the far end of it to look out a window. He whirled away from the window now and came

74

back to the kitchen part, where Aunt Sue and Uncle Tucker were dancing.

"Somebody's coming. Get Tucker into the bedroom."

Aunt Sue stopped dancing and tried to take Uncle Tucker by the arm. He got away from her and picked up the glass of whisky and downed a big gulp of it. He then started for one of the bedrooms. Aunt Sue followed.

Pa had gone to another window. After a moment, he turned and called, "It's all right. It's Elwood."

Pa opened the back door and Mr. Snowe came in. Stevie had met him the day they arrived. He patted Stevie on the shoulder.

"How are you, son?" To Pa he said, "You getting settled in all right?"

Uncle Tucker came out of the bedroom, singing and waltzing. He grabbed Mr. Snowe and tried to dance with him. Mr. Snowe got away from him and put the kitchen table between them. Uncle Tucker pulled a chair out from the table. He turned it around backward and tried to sit down astraddle of it, but he got tangled in his skirt and crashed to the floor along with the chair.

"Good God, Sip" Mr. Snowe said. "You promised you'd control his drinking. If anybody should drop in—"

"Shut up, Elwood," Pa said. "I am controlling his drinking. He didn't touch a drop all the time we were on the road. I knew this was coming and I planned for it. There'll be maybe another day of it, maybe not even that. Then he'll be all right for a spell."

Uncle Tucker got himself untangled and into a

chair. Aunt Susan came in from the bedroom. She had the glass that had been full of whisky. It was now empty.

"You'd better listen to me, Sip," Mr. Snowe said. "The county sheriff is at the phalanstery right now."

That jolted Pa. He stared at Mr. Snowe stonily. Before he could speak, Mr. Snowe went on.

"I don't know what he wants. There's no reason to think it has anything to do with you. But if Tucker got loose right now—"

"He ain't going to get loose. I thought you said the sheriff didn't come poking around here."

"He doesn't ordinarily. The last time he was here was about a year ago. He came to ask about some stray cattle. I imagine it's like that this time."

Pa went to a window and stood there staring, his mouth open as if he had a bad taste in it. "I don't see how it could be about us."

"I don't either."

"Only thing would be if somebody followed Susanna. If that was so, it seems like they would have come down on us when it was camped out of town. She would have led 'em right to us."

"Nobody followed me," Susanna said. She stood behind the chair Uncle Tucker was in. She laid an arm across his shoulders. He put his head against her and closed his eyes. She added, "I told you about that Mayberly."

"Mayberly" Sip said. "I never saw him close up, far as I know. If I ever do—"

"Well, he had got wind of the Grizzly Creek place," she said. "He was pretty sure of himself too. He hung around Dos Pinos for a few days but he was gone before I left. And I don't see how anybody could trace me. I bought a stage ticket to Fort Collins, like you told me to. I pretended to the driver that I had made a mistake and got him to exchange it."

"You notice anybody suspicious along the way? Somebody riding the same coach maybe?"

She shook her head. "I was on three different coaches and I made two stopovers. I'd have noticed anyone following me. And I was the only passenger to get off at Spinnerville."

Pa nodded and seemed satisfied. He said, "Just the same, I'd feel better if you find out what that sheriff has on his mind, Elwood."

"I'll try. Favra is damned closemouthed."

Uncle Tucker had gone to sleep. Pa and Aunt Sue got him to his feet and half-carried him to a bedroom. Mr. Snowe bustled around the table and sat down in the chair Uncle Tucker had been in.

"How do you like it here, boy?"

"All right," Stevie said.

"You'll like it fine when you get used to it. Your father will make a place for himself here. All the bad things from the past will be forgotten. You'll have a good life, a good life."

Pa came back from the bedroom. Mr. Snowe said, "Sip, it's time to talk. Privately."

"I don't hide nothing from the boy," Pa said.

"I want to go over the whole thing from beginning to end, Sip." Mr. Snowe smiled at Stevie. "This is grown-up talk, boy."

Stevie went into the bedroom where they had taken Uncle Tucker, who was stretched out now, dead to the world. Aunt Sue sat on the edge of the bed with her chin in her hands. She gave a little shrug and said, "Hallelujah!"

Stevie's bedroom was a small room that could be reached only by going through this one. He went into it now. The one small window had been nailed shut except for an inch at the top. Pa had done this from the outside. It would be impossible to get out the window without breaking the glass and making a noise.

The room was at the back end of the house, next to the kitchen with only a thin board wall between. Stevie's bunk was built against this wall. He lay down on it and could hear Mr. Snowe's voice clearly. He guessed Pa knew he could hear, too, if he wanted to, and didn't care. Pa had said once that he already knew more than enough to hang them, so what did another earful matter? Stevie wondered if he was an outlaw, too, now. He wondered what would happen to him if they all got caught.

"...too many fool risks," Mr. Snowe was saying. "I don't understand why the boy is here. It would have been better to get him later."

"It don't matter to me if you understand or not," Pa said. "He is my son. He was being raised by a old-maid dressmaker who would teach him his pa is the scum of the earth. He's getting used to me and he will be all right. Susanna will be good for him. I give him a pretty good whomping right at first when he didn't do like he was told. He'll remember it. And I told him I would kill his aunt if he tried to go back. I could let him run loose right now and he wouldn't run off. I won't do it, not for a time yet, but I could."

"All right," Snowe said. "But we ought to move fast as we can. When I'm head of the colony, we'll all be safe.''

"We could move *too* fast, Elwood.''

"I'm going to be president of New Sanity before this summer is over, Sip. I've made up my mind to it. I've been going over the plan and I've made some refinements.''

"Just so I know *everything*, Elwood. You had better not hold back any surprises like you did on that stage office job.''

"I don't know what you're talking about,'' Snowe said.

"You're a liar. You were a two-bit clerk and not getting anyplace. You tipped Fletch off to that gold shipment and he got in touch with me and Tuck. But you and Fletch had a private deal we didn't know about. You promised him a thousand dollars out of your share if he would kill the agent during the hold-up. You wanted his job and his wife. You got 'em both, thanks to Fletch. But you couldn't hold onto either one, could you, Elwood?''

"Believe that if you want to,'' Mr. Snowe said. "It's all in the past. I'm not going to argue about it.''

"It wouldn't be in the past if Tucker and me was to be taken, Elwood.''

"If you're taken, it will be because of Tucker's drinking. Or because of the boy.''

"And if we was to be taken dead, you wouldn't have nothing to worry about.''

There was a sharp sound as if someone had slapped the table. Then a chair scraped and it seemed as if Mr. Snowe had got up and moved away from the table. His voice was a little fainter.

"You're a poor mind reader,'' he said.

"We saw Fletch on the way here. He gave us a little help. We knew we could trust him. Up to a point."

There was a pause. Then Mr. Snowe said uncertainly, "How is he?"

"Well, I read his mind, too, you might say. That time I was right. Leastways, we was ready when he tried to kill us. Fletch is dead now, Elwood."

"Sip—"

"He died of miscalculation, you might say."

Stevie remembered Fltech's limp body as they rolled it into the grave. A man could be alive and full of schemes one minute and a sodden meaningless thing the next. He thought how Mr. Snowe would look dead. Or Pa. Or Uncle Tucker. He didn't want anybody to be dead.

"You're right, Sip," Mr. Snowe said. "There mustn't be any miscalculation. On my part or on yours."

"I just wanted to hear you say it," Pa said. "And the money. We're going to share that right down the middle. I want to hear you say that too."

"Right down the middle."

"How much you think there'll be, Elwood?"

"More than you ever dreamed of. Once we run those Shakers out, we'll sell off their land piece by piece. It's damned good land now that it's irrigated. If we sell it cheap and fast, we'll raise a hundred thousand in a hurry. Maybe more."

"How long will it take to run them out?"

"If we build it up right, it should be done by fall. We ought to start right away. The first thing will be to blast Patrol headquarters, as I told you. I'll try to stir up the right climate for that within the next few days.

The Patrol will be quick enough to blame the Shakers. Favra will be slow to speak out against them, but we'll push until he does. We'll blast the phalanstery. He'll be angry then. He'll have to be killed in a way that makes a martyr of him and puts the blame squarely on the Shakers. From there on, it will be up to me. I'll take over. I'll have plenty of backing and we'll run them out.''

"Well, I guess you know these people and how they will think,'' Pa said. "You had better be right. What about the dynamite?''

"I went up to Star City and got it last week. Favra's been talking about changing the course of a creek up in the high country. He's been talking about it for years. He claims that a little blasting in the right places will turn the creek into a new channel and it will join the river. I persuaded him that now's the time to do it and I got permission to order the dynamite. It's stored up at the dam now. I'm going up there now and I'm going to report to Favra that a case is missing.''

~~sing.''~~

"You've already swiped it?'' Pa asked.

"It's in a gunny sack under your back porch,'' Mr. Snowe said.

Mayberly was gone from Spinnerville for four days. When he returned, he put up his tired horse at the livery and went at once to the sheriff's office.

The sheriff was doing his paper work. He looked up over his glasses and moaned.

"Nothing,'' Mayberly said. "I stopped at every way station, every ranch, every bunkhouse. Nobody's seen that wagon party. They couldn't have gone north.''

"You're saying they're right here in my lap some-where?''

"It looks like it.''

'I checked the colony. Favra says he's had no new arrivals since the fourteenth.''

"You believe him?''

"I don't know. He doesn't want me nosing around out there. He made that a little too clear. He isn't the kind of man you call a liar, though.''

"I'll get some sleep,'' Mayberly said. "I'll have a look out there tomorrow.''

"You ought to be told about the little constabulary they have out there. They call it the Patrol. Tough bunch.''

"What's their legal status?''

"Damned if I know. Within the township, they're legal enough, I suppose. But they have no authority outside of that area. They're not county deputies.''

"Then they'd better not lean on me outside the township.''

"Wait a minute,'' the sheriff said. "Let me tell you about these boys. A few years back, half a dozen young cowpokes were pestering the women out there. The Patrol rounded 'em up. Next day every one of those cowpokes left the county. Every one. Few months ago, I ran into one of 'em and found out what happened. Seems the Patrol took those boys up into the hills, stripped 'em naked, and drove them out of town. The boys never came back.''

Mayberly grunted. "Nice people.''

"My formal and official advice is to stay the hell away from New Sanity,'' the sheriff said. "I don't

82

imagine you're going to follow it. All I can do is make certain you know what you'll be up against."

"Obliged."

"Don't mention it. Your lady friend is at the hotel. Got in day before yesterday. You didn't tell me there would be a man with her."

The sheriff was watching Mayberly with a close interest and maybe a hint of amusement. Mayberly met the appraisal grimly.

"A man? I'll be damned."

"Came in on the same coach. Fellow named Deeds. Clean-cut, well-dressed type. Claims to work for the N.P. Says he's here to make a survey of the area. There's a possibility the road will build a spur down this way, he says."

"You'd expect an N.P. man to travel by railroad," Mayberly said. "But this one arrived by stage from the other direction."

"Just between us gateposts, he has nothing to do with the N.P. He dropped in and identified himself to me. I may be violating a confidence, but I reckon you'd guess the truth anyway. He's a Pinkerton man."

Forty-six miles southeast of Spinnerville in the bunkhouse of a cattle outfit called the Dancing D. Harry Yadkin stretched out on a borrowed bunk and went over the map he had in his mind. He had never been in this country before, but he had painstakingly collected information about the way and wasn't likely to get lost. Sip and Tucker Ambrose were north of here somewhere. He was sure of that. He also knew that Tucker was wearing woman's clothing, that the boy was with them, and that they were traveling in a wagon and leading three saddle horses.

After Mayberly had set him afoot, he walked to the town of McFadden. The town marshal had been sympathetic and had lent him a horse so he could go back and retrieve his cached gear. He had hitched a ride to Medicine Bow with a nester and his wife. There he had got a backbreaking, dollar-a-day job at a hay and grain barn. He had got a five-dollar advance on his wages and got into the saloon's two-bit poker game. He had bottom-dealt himself into a fifteen-dollar winning streak, had quit the job, paid back the advance, and got into the game again the next night.

It was at Medicine Bow that he saw the item in the newspaper. It was a three-inch item at the bottom of the front page. It said that a farmer named Joseph Kirkland had disappeared near Sheridan and that a search for him was under way.

Yadkin knew Joseph Kirkland. In fact, he had known him back in Durango when he had gone under the name of Joseph Fletcher and had hung around with the wild bunch that included the Ambrose boys. A couple of years ago, Yadkin's old partner, dead now, had discovered that Fletch was farming up near Sheridan and had changed his name. They had wondered about that because, as far as they knew, he wasn't wanted by the law except maybe for questioning. So they had gone up there and done a little questioning on their own. They had learned nothing from Fletch but had come away with the idea that he might possibly still be in touch with Sip and Tucker.

So the newspaper item was mighty interesting.

Yadkin graduated to the Medicine Bow saloon's fifty-cent game. He had taken long chances and had been lucky. Not in the way the cards fell—luck had little to do with that. He had been lucky that his bottom deal went undetected. It was hardly of fifty-cent-game quality and he knew it.

He had won enough to buy a horse that would get him to Sheridan. He had arrived a day before bloodhounds led a posse to Fletch's grave near the deserted cabin a few miles north of town. The sheriff had traced Fletch's movements prior to the murder. The information was discussed all over town. Yadkin did a little questioning on his own and gathered additional details. He learned that Fletch had bought a good team and a wagon. He had covered the wagon with an old tarp. He had bought a supply of food and clothing. Strangely, some of it was women's clothing.

From a deputy, Yadkin learned that a farmer a few miles south of the cabin had talked to a suspicious-looking man who was cutting across his property. There had been a boy with the man. The farmer had asked them to get a doctor. The man had said he would, but he did not. A doctor had eventually arrived. The woman had appendicitis, he said. He had operated on the kitchen table. But he was too late. A few days later the farmer's wife died of peritonitis. The farmer was very bitter toward the stranger. He described him in detail for Yadkin, right down to light blue eyes and heavy black stubble. Yadkin knew for sure that he was onto Sip Ambrose then.

After Fletch's body had been dug up and reinterred in the Sheridan cemetary, Yadkin had visited the cabin. Most of the signs had been obliterated by that time, of course. But by riding a wide circle around the place he had picked up the tracks of the wagon and the three saddle horses. He had followed the tracks to where they entered the road and had seen that the party had turned north.

Trailing that wagon had been a tedious business. There were days when he found no one at all who had seen the party and he was afraid he had lost it. The task of tracing it would have been next to hopeless if it hadn't been for the three saddle horses that were trailing along. He had found more than one man who could tell him the color and size of those horses but who didn't remember the people in the wagon at all.

Here at Dancing D he had had a bit of solid luck. The party had borrowed a forge and reset a shoe on one of the harness horses. The woman and the boy had remained in the wagon, but several of the cowhands had talked to the man. He looked like a Quaker, they said, but he wasn't. He cussed too much. One of them remembered that he had asked how far it was to Spinnerville.

That might mean that Spinnerville was their destination or that they were going beyond it. It might even have been a deliberate effort on Sip's part to leave a false trail. But Yadkin didn't think so. Far from their usual stamping ground and with Tucker dressed as a woman, Sip was probably feeling pretty secure.

It had taken Yadkin a while to figure out about Tucker. But once he thought of it, he was sure he was right. Yadkin was one of the few persons hunting the Ambrose boys who had seen them face to face. Tucker was small and slight. He was quarter-breed Cheyenne and didn't have much beard. And when you considered the clothing Fletch had bought—a dress, a bonnet, shoes, and stockings—the only explanation that made any sense was that they were a disguise for Tucker. And now one of the Dancing-D hands had confirmed it. The woman in the wagon was very dark, he remembered. She looked as if she might have Indian blood.

Yadkin sighed comfortably and turned on his side. He would get a good night's sleep and be on his way again right after breakfast.

9

MELODY COATES was making herself a dress. For her, this was merely a matter of a few hours of concentrated effort. She had found the material at a Spinnerville store. It was a patterned silk, a little wild and exotic and not really practical. The design was a simple one. She had cut it out without a pattern. She had quickly stitched the dress together and now was working on a wide belt of the same material that she hoped would add a touch of smartness.

She had thoroughly enjoyed the long trip from Fort Collins. The weather was not yet warm enough to make stage travel uncomfortable. The scenery was spectacular. But the really exciting thing was the company of Mr. Benjamin Deeds.

She had first noticed him at the Laramie railroad station when, following the instructions in Mayberly's note, she had begun her trip to Fort Collins. Mr. Deeds had taken the same train. He, too, had changed to the Denver train at Cheyenne. She had got off at Fort Collins and checked into the Rocky Mountain Hotel. When she went to breakfast the next morning, there he was in the dining room. It came to her then that he was very likely following her. As if he could read her mind, he came to her table, introduced himself, and admitted it.

He was not at all what she would have expected a detective to be like. He was under thirty, spoke grammatically, and had very nice manners. He was tastefully dressed in a gray suit, white shirt, and a blue tie that matched his eyes. His neat dark hair had just a touch of a wave in it. He was lively company and a most attractive man.

There was no sense in lying to him. He knew that she was Melody Coates and not Mrs. George Russell, as she had registered. He had been assigned to watch her, to contact her if that seemed feasible. He had caught up with her in Laramie. He knew that she had had dinner with Mayberly. He also knew that a bounty hunter named Yadkin had been in Laramie and had followed Mayberly out of town. Mr. Deeds had decided to stick with Melody. When she had suddenly bought a railroad ticket, he guessed that Mayberly had drawn Yadkin out of town so she could get away.

"Mayberly probably led him off and tried to lose him," he said. "If that failed, one of them has quite possibly killed the other by this time."

He seemed to consider that amusing. Melody did not, but she found herself returning his smile.

"And you're waiting here for Mayberly," he said.

She smiled again and said nothing.

"No reason why you shouldn't admit it," Mr. Deeds said. "I'll find out eventually, won't I?"

"I'm not going to talk about my plans, Mr. Deeds."

"Come, now. I know about Mayberly, although he doesn't know me. Our men have tangled with him from time to time and there's a brief Pinkerton report on him. He's obsessed with the idea of taking the

89

Ambrose brothers on his own. Obsessed. He's unprincipled, dangerous. He's interested only in the reward, not in your nephew's well-being."

"He told me as much," Melody said. "He even warned me that he might use me as bait."

"Well, there you are," Mr. Deeds said gaily. "The only thing to do is to sell him out completely."

"You sound a little unprincipled yourself."

"Come, now. You'll be much better off co-operating with me—with the Pinkerton organization. We're certainly much more likely to find your nephew than a lone-wolf bounty hunter."

That sounded quite sensible. After all, the only consideration was to do the best thing for Stevie. But Mayberly had seemed to understand that. He had said the boy's safety came before anything else. She was not ready to sell Mayberly out.

"The truth is I couldn't sell him out if I wanted to," she said. "I don't know what he's up to. He told me to wait here until I hear from him. That's all."

"Fair enough. We'll wait together."

She gave him no encouragement, but he took it upon himself to see that she was not bored. They had lunch and dinner together every day. He insisted on paying the check. It would go on his expense account, he said. He hired a buggy and took her for a drive through the colorfully historic country around the town. They picnicked in a mountain meadow, panned for gold along the Cache la Poudre, and had a moment of excitement when she washed some yellow mica. He occasionally asked a question or two about the Ambrose brothers but he certainly didn't badger her.

Mayberly's letter came on the fourth day. It contained a hundred dollars and instructions to take a train to Rock Springs and then go north by stage to Spinnerville, Montana. This was so suprisingly far from where she would expect to find the Ambrose brothers that she was tempted to discuss the letter with Mr. Deeds. But there was something about Mayberly that she had liked, something she trusted. Besides, she was spending his money. She said nothing about the letter. She checked out of the hotel just before train time. She was sure that Mr. Deeds hadn't seen her leave. She had a three-hour layover in Denver, however, and when her westbound train was called, there he was at the gate.

There was a gay dinner on the U.P. diner with roast squab and a half bottle of white Bordeaux. They arrived at Rock Springs before noon the next day and began the long stage ride north. Mr. Deeds was interested in everything and made the trip into an adventure. One evening at a way station they had walked to the top of a ridge and looked down on a sage-dappled valley in purple twilight. Their hands touched and he drew her to him and kissed her. It seemed right at first; then he became altogether too ardent. He seemed to have the idea that they were going to become lovers right then and there. She set him straight in a hurry hoping she didn't seem too old-maidish about it.

She was on her guard after that. She had to get Stevie back. She didn't trust herself to think straight about anything until she had done that. She certainly wasn't going to mix things up by having a romance with one of Mr. Pinkerton's detectives.

And now they were in this funny, barnlike Spinnerville hotel. The lobby was three stories high and the rooms opened off two balconies that ran all the way around it. Both of them had rooms on the second floor. His was directly across the way from hers with the width of the lobby between them. She was being silly probably, but every time she entered or left her room, she had a feeling that he knew it. It was as if he had bored a peephole in his door and did nothing but stare through it.

What really bothered her, of course, was what Mr. Mayberly would do when he found out about Mr. Deeds. She told herself that there had been nothing she could do about it and that Mr. Mayberly would understand. But she wasn't sure. She wasn't sure of anything about Mr. Mayberly. From her first sight of him that day in Laramie, a dark figure out of the storm, she had sometimes thought of him as a little unreal, a sort of angry angel who was a law unto himself.

She was stitching the belt to the dress. It would be a wide, tight circle that trimmed her waist from hips to bust. To get it exactly right was a tricky bit of sewing that absorbed her entire attention. The knock on the door startled her.

She knew before she opened it that Mayberly would be there. He was—big and unshaven and dusty-looking. He pushed into the room and closed the door. The foreknowledge of his appearance had been so certain that she was frightened. She tried to assure herself that there was nothing clairvoyant about it. Perhaps she remembered his knock from the time he had knocked in Laramie. Perhaps she had subconsciously heard his step in the hall and remembered that. In any case, she had been thinking about him only a moment ago. But might not that in itself be more than coincidence?

"I'm glad to see you," she said shakily.

"Sit down," he said. "Tell me about this Deeds."

She was surprised that he knew but a little relieved too. At least she wouldn't have to fumble around for a gentle way to break the news. She moved the dress to one side and sat down on the bed.

"Are you angry?" she said.

"Tell me, please. The whole thing."

His icy politeness said that he was very angry indeed. She sighed and began the story, trying not to sound defensive. He listened restlessly, now and then pacing to the window and glaring into the street. When she has finished, he positioned a chair to suit him and sat down.

"I may be onto something," he said. "I can't make it fit together very well, but I may be close to locating your nephew. I said *may*. The situation is damned touchy— especially so because I'm not as clear on it as I'd like to be. One mistake and we'll lose everything. I've been close before and I know how easily that can happen."

"I can't blame you because Deeds is here," he went on. "I should have spotted him in Laramie. But you've got friendly with him. I want to know now which of us you're working with. It can't be both."

"I don't understand why not," Melody said. "I should think you and he might work together. You're both after the same thing."

"All right, you don't understand. Just take my word for it. You have to choose. And I'll lay it on the line, Miss Coates. If you choose me, I'm going to ask you to mislead Deeds, lie to him."

"To send him off on a wild-goose chase so you can have the reward all to yourself?"

"Yes, ma'am."

"That is completely ridiculous, Mr. Mayberly."

He got to his feet. "Then you're working with the Pinkerton people. Good-by, Miss Coates."

"Wait. I don't know what to say. I took your money."

"Call it a bad bet on my part," he said.

"And I owe you more than money." She had got to her feet; now she sank down on the bed again. She wished he would sit down too. "You came along when I was badly discouraged. You gave me a glimmer of hope. I can't tell you how badly I needed that just then."

"If you feel guilty about the money, call it a loan," Mayberly said. He moved toward the door. "Send it to me sometime."

"Wait," she said again. "What kind of lie do you want me to tell?"

"Does it make any difference? A lie's a lie."

"You make it awfully hard. I feel as if I've betrayed you. Now you want me to betray Mr. Deeds. Is there no other way?"

"No."

"The sheriff came by to see me the other day. He said you were up north. Are Sip and Stevie up there somewhere?"

Mayberly smiled tiredly. "You can't really believe I'd answer that, Miss Coates. Not if you're on the Pinkerton side of the fence."

"You're impossible!"

"Yes, ma'am. This will be done my way or not at all. I

thought I made that clear at the beginning."

Melody bit back her temper. She had to admit that what he said was true enough. He had been candid with her and more than fair. It was just that he seemed incapable of being fair with anyone else. And he did seem to have some kind of a lead. Mr. Deeds had nothing.

"Very well," she said. "I'll tell your lie for you. What do you want me to say?"

He took a folded paper from his pocket and handed it to her. He went back to his chair and sat down. He suddenly seemed very tired.

"Tell Deeds that's a letter you got from me. Don't let him know I'm in town."

She folded the paper. The date line was Three Forks, Montana. The letter said that Sip and Tucker Ambrose and Stevie were definitely up there in Madison County. When he had them pinpointed and was ready to move, he would send for her. In the meantime, she was to stay where she was.

Melody sighed and lowered the letter to her lap. "He'll read this and head for Three Forks. Is that the idea?... But he knows you. If he sees you in town, he'll realize the letter is a—hoax."

"He was in the bar drinking a bottle of Gilbert's beer when I came up here. He didn't see me. Before I leave, I want you to make sure he's still there. If he isn't, find him and occupy his attention till I can get out of the hotel. I've got a room at a boardinghouse—Mrs. Torgenson's on Spinner Street. As soon as he's left town, let me know."

Mayberly dined on Mrs. Torgenson's roast pork and dressing in quantities that had the other boarders looking askance at him. He then monopolized the bathroom for a full hour while he soaked in the tin bathtub. Then he returned to his room, went to bed, and slept a solid ten hours.

He was wakened by persistent knocking and saw that the sun was streaming in his windows. He pulled on his pants and found the sheriff at the door. There was a stranger with him.

"Wish I could lie abed mornings," the sheriff said as they came into the room. "My wife won't stand for it, even on Sundays. Mr. Mayberly, this is Mr. Asbury."

Mayberly and the stranger shook hands. He was a very short man, barely five feet, but of a staunch, broad-shouldered build. He had a square face framed by long gray sideburns. He wore overalls over a gray flannel shirt. He carried a battered derby hat in his hand.

"Mr. Asbury if from the colony," the sheriff explained. "He's a Shaker by faith. They've had a little trouble out there. A dynamiting."

"Obfisticated the guardhouse," Mr. Asbury added.

"That's what they call the Patrol's headquarters," the sheriff explained. "It's a three-room building off to itself half a mile north of the other community buildings. Or was. It seems that there were two members of the Patrol on duty and, for a miracle, neither was seriously hurt."

"They was at t'other end of the building from that which was obfisticated," Mr. Asbury said. "They got a bit of a bounce, is all."

"This happened night before last," the sheriff said, "and this is the first I've heard of it. It's plain that

Favra doesn't consider it any of the county's business. On the other hand, Mr. Asbury says the Patrol is blaming the Shakers. He and a few others are worried and decided to notify me. So I'm betwixt the devil and the deep. Thought I'd ask you to help me out. You're not known out there and folks aren't likely to associate you with the county. And under the circumstances I thought you might be interested."

"Yesterday your formal and official advice was to stay the hell away from there," Mayberly said.

"It's still good advice. But now you'll have the co-operation of Mr. Asbury here and one or two of his friends. You'll pretend to be a cousin of his, dropping by for a visit."

"I hope the others will agree the deception is acceptable in the eyes of the Lord," Mr. Asbury said. "I reckon they'll want to pray over it."

"What if they don't agree?" Mayberly asked.

"Well, they won't turn you in, but they won't help you none, either. But I reckon they'll agree. We are in a monstracious situation out there."

"You'll have a deputy's badge in your pocket," the sheriff said. "I hope you won't have to fall back on it, but you'll have it."

The plan was a good one, and Mayberly regarded the sheriff with increased respect. The man couldn't openly investigate without antagonizing the colony's leader. The possible political consequences might be disastrous for him and every other county official. Yet it might be just as disastrous for him to turn his back on the situation, especially since Mr. Asbury had come to him. To send a man out there undercover seemed a sensible solution to the dilemma.

"Mightn't it seem a little careless to give a badge to a stranger?" Mayberly asked.

"I'm not a careless man," the sheriff said. "I was curious about that letter you carry, so a few days ago I wrote a telegram to H. B. Tovey. I sent a deputy up to Star City to send it. The southbound stage brought an answer yesterday. You can wear a badge in my county any time it suits you, Mr. Mayberly."

"I hope we can keep this all on the q.t.," Mr. Asbury said. "There are plenty of my people who don't want nothing whatever to do with worldly institutions, including deputies."

10

MAYBERLY AND Mr. Asbury rode side by side into the north end of Singing Valley, the Shaker end. Mr. Asbury's young jenny mule had developed unabashed affection for Mayberly's gelding and kept nuzzling it—to the embarrassment of both the horse and Mr. Asbury, who was too one-track to talk and control his animal at the same time. Right now, talking was more important; so Mayberly kept his cussing silent and put up with the nuzzling.

"Us Believers who stayed on here ain't the best of the old colony, religiously speakin'," Asbury said. "Those that truly had the Spirit up and absquatulated when they learned about Dr. Favra's male and female notions. Me, I do my work, go to meetin', and I'm an elder now, the which I would never have been in the old days. I believe in the Comin' and in the quaternity, but I ain't got the Spirit the way some gets it. I try to make myself useful by lookin' after the worldy things that has got to be done.

"Us Believers is in a touchy position here. We're kind of a community within a community, you might say. We hold onto our old ways best we can and try to fit ourselves into Favra's organization too. He figures us for addled, I reckon, but by and large he's been fair with us. That ain't true for some of the other folks up around the phalanstery. The Patrol has always been just plain mean. We don't believe in dispute. We try to meet hostiltiy with kindness,

99

and that just seems to egg 'em on.

"Those of us who stayed on there have backslid in some ways. We eat meat and we use tobacco. Those are things which the Believers did in the days of Mother Ann, though they was forbidden later, and we don't feel they're specially offensive to the Spirit. We do practice celibacy and we take pride in good works and we lean over backward to be honest. I reckon that all has a holier-than-thou sound to it. So when one of our people does give in to the devil in some way, it looks worse than it would if we didn't set our sights so high. We're all called hypocrites and fakers. Especially by the Patrol.

"The present trouble commenced a few days ago when the Patrol come around to search our buildings. They claimed there was a box of dynamite stole from some place and we had it. When they didn't find nothing, they got mean and began the search all over again, tearin' things up and makin' a mess. We went around and tidied up and never raised our voices and they got meaner'n ever. If you are immersed in the Spirit, Mr. Mayberly, it don't matter none what happens to you in this world. But if you ain't teetotaciously immersed, if you are like me and still care a little something about your rights and the rights of your people, you are better off to take a stand. That is what me and one or two others tried to do. We ordered the Patrol away from our buildings. When they wouldn't leave, Philander Hotchkiss, who is a member of the New Sanity council, went and saw Dr. Favra. The Patrol was called off."

"Well, like you know, night before last the guardhouse was obfisticated with dynamite. So the Patrol come back. All day yesterday it was questioning Believers. Anybody who spoke up pert was likely to get roughed up. Philander went to see Favra again. This time he said the Patrol was a necessary evil and we'd have to put up with it. It looks like he thinks Believers done the dynamiting, Philander says. So Philander and me decided I ought to go and notify the sheriff on the q.t.... '

They followed a wagon trace between fields of gold-tinged wheat and reached a neat and well-arranged little settlement. There was a straight, wide street and a smaller one that intersected it at a right angle. There was a large brick two-story house at the intersection. Other buildings were joined by brick-bordered paths that made a trim pattern on the grassy quadrants. Asbury called the large building the ''dwelling,'' and he pointed out others—a meetinghouse, barns, a brick shop and kiln, a blacksmith shop, a warehouse.

''We have four such centers,'' Mr. Asbury said, ''the which we call 'families.' This here is called the Asbury family, account of I'm in charge of it. Almost fifty people. We all live in the same building, men downstairs and women upstairs. You'll stay in the guesthouse. I'll be introducin' you to folks, so I'll have to know your Christian name. We use only Christian names except sometimes for elders and such.''

''It's Zack.''

''I take it that's for Zachariah. We never use nicknames.''

''Zachariah.''

''Mine's Stephen. We'll stop by the guesthouse and you can leave your saddlebags. Your guns too.''

''I'll keep the guns.''

''It will be frowned on.''

''There may be an aspect to this matter you're not aware of,'' Mayberly said. ''I'll keep 'em.''

Mr. Asbury accepted that with a sour look and a shrug. They dismounted in front of the guesthouse and went inside. It was a small, low building with six cots in the men's section. The mattresses were rolled and there were no sheets or blankets in evidence. It was plain that Mayberly would be the only guest.

A chubby little man hurried up to them as they left the building. He turned out to be Philander Hotchkiss, whom Asbury had mentioned earlier. He eyed Mayberly doubtfully while Asbury explained the sheriff's plan.

"I don't know, I don't know," Philander Hotchkiss said. "I was hoping the sheriff might go to Dr. Favra and persuade him to call off the Patrol. Something like that."

"Maybe that will come later," Asbury said. "Maybe Mr. Mayberly will find evidence that points at the guilty people."

"I don't know, I don't know," Hotchkiss said.

"Myself, I don't see what's to do but go ahead," Asbury said. "It's the only plan we got."

"I shan't oppose it," Hotchkiss said. "But I wash my hands of it. I leave it up to thee, Stephen."

Remembering that Philander Hotchkiss was on the New Sanity council, Mayberly asked him a question that he had asked earlier and that Asbury hadn't been able to answer.

"Do you know of a new family that joined the colony about a week ago? There was probably a man, two women, and a child. They probably would have arrived in a wagon with three horses in tow."

"Well, there was the Johnsons," Hotchkiss said. "I don't know about the horses, but I believe there are four in the family. Ony two were introduced to the council. They have a house in the upper part of the valley."

"Is one of the women young with dark eyes and hair, pretty?"

Mr. Hotchkiss looked uncomfortable. Mayberly realized it was probably an error to ask if he considered a woman pretty.

"I'm sure there are two females," Hotchkiss said. "One was ill, as was the boy. Something like that. I'm quite sure, quite sure. They were given some special privileges. The colony built the house for them. Mr. Johnson paid for it. He also turned a tidy little sum over to the colony. Five thousand dollars."

"I know the house," Asbury said. "Several Believers worked on it. I didn't know it was now occupied."

"I'll want you to take me there," Mayberly said.

"It's a long ride. This valley is nigh unto thirty miles long."

"We'll have a look at the guardhouse first."

"If I may say so," Philander Hotchkiss said, "if I may say so, I was a little surprised that the Johnsons were given so much consideration. They struck me as ordinary farm folk and not the very worldly type that Dr. Favra goes out of his way to recruit. Probably the temporal consideration— the five thousand dollars—explains it."

"I have another question, Mr. Hotchkiss," Mayberly said. "How can you be certain that none of your people had anything to do with that dynamiting?"

"We avoid violence under all conditions. That is a basic tenet of our religion. During the Civil War, we refused military service and were pardoned by President Lincoln. Those of us who were converted after serving in a war refuse pensions. Anyone who speaks to another human being in anger is guilty of a sin that must be publicly confessed. We do not even wear spurs. Buggy whips beyond a certain length and weight are forbidden. To strike out against the Patrol with dynamite is entirely out of keeping with our nature."

"Yet the Patrol thinks your people are guilty."

"They are trying to put the blame on us, yes."

"I want you to go around and question your people," Mayberly said. "Make a real effort to find out if anyone knows anything or suspects anything."

"We've done that," Hotchkiss said. "The explosion took place after a general meeting at our large meeting-house, which is a way north of here, there miles from the guardhouse. Most of our people were on their way home when they heard it. The northernmost 'family' was just arriving at their home area. A few of them turned their wagons around and went to investigate."

"All right," Mayberly said, "but keep trying. If there's any guilt among your people, it's best that you know it first."

It was almost time for the midday meal and they waited for it before setting out. It was served in a large dining hall with men and women eating at separate tables. All knelt in silent prayer before sitting down to eat. The food was starchy and plentiful. There was no conversation at table, no talk beyond, "Please pass the butter." When everyone had finished, there was another moment of kneeling before they left the building.

The ride to the guardhouse took a full hour. One end of the small narrow brick building was demolished completely. The rest was badly enough damaged so that the Patrol had set up headquarters in a small wall tent. Two men came out of the tent as Mayberly and Mr. Asbury rode up. They were dressed alike in black boots and trousers, blue shirts, and black hats. Both wore gunbelts with revolvers in open holsters. One of the men was barely out of his teens. The other was a few years older and wore a big oxbow mustache with waxed points.

"What have we here?" he asked, his eyes on Mayberly. "When did Shakers take to packing weapons?"

Mayberly dismounted and turned away from the man. He walked over to the building to inspect the damage.

"Mister, I asked you a question," the man with the mustache said.

"A foolish question," Mayberly said.

"Captain Hosko, this here is a visitor," Mr. Asbury said quickly. "My cousin Zachariah from Colorado."

"You registered him at the phalanstery?" Captain Hosko demanded.

"What do you figure?" Mayberly said, nodding at the ruins of the building. "Ten sticks?"

"Two dozen sticks, at least. All visitors must be registered immediately upon arrival."

"The charge was set in two places," Mayberly said. "It was expertly placed. I'd say five sticks in each bundle."

"You got an uppity way about you," Hosko said. "I got a notion to take you into custody. We got orders from Mr. Snowe to bring in anybody suspicious. He will interrogate them himself."

Mayberly turned to Asbury. "Snowe? Who's that?"

"He's the vice-president."

"Snowe. He got a first name?"

"Elwood. Mr. Elwood Snowe."

"I'll be damned," Mayberly said. "He spell Snowe with an *e* on the end?"

"Yes, he does," Asbury said. "You know him?"

A man wasn't likely to run into two men named Elwood

Snowe in a lifetime. But Mayberly replied cautiously. "I don't know. How long has he been in the colony?"

Asbury pondered a moment. "He's been vice-president a little more'n a year, I guess. He come here two, three years before that. Got on the council right away. He come up fast."

"He's a damn smart man," Hosko said.

Mayberly took a last look at the remains of the guard-house. "Let's go," he said to Asbury. "Let's get that registering done."

As they rode off, he said, "That was for the captain's benefit. One thing I don't want right now is to be seen by Elwood Snowe. Can you go in and register me while I keep out of sight?"

"I guess so," Asbury said. "Snowe would recognize you?"

"He would," Mayberly said. "He would also recognize my name. As long as I'm supposed to be your cousin, register me as Zachariah Asbury."

Asbury sighed. "Seems like when you get involved with falsehood, there's no end to it. When this is over, I'm goin' to have a lot to confess in meetin'."

They were quickly in sight of the phalanstery and the buildings surrounding it. They parted company then, with Mayberly swinging to the east to put a low hill between him and the buildings. He dismounted in the shade of a cottonwood to wait. It was almost an hour before Asbury showed up, wagging his head and looking worried.

"They got some of my 'family' at the phalanstery," he said. "They are waiting to be questioned. The Patrol is guarding them."

"Are they holding any others—any who aren't Shakers?" Mayberly asked. He was sitting against the tree trunk. He stretched and yawned without getting to his feet.

"Not that I seen."

"I've been sitting here puzzling," Mayberly said. "There seem to be two puzzles with the pieces all mixed together. But maybe that isn't so. Maybe the pieces all fit together after all."

Asbury stared down from his saddle, his eyes wide. "I can't say as I follow your drift. You care to explaterate?"

Mayberly got to his feet and stretched again. His horse was eying the affectionate mule and edging away. Mayberly caught up the reins and swung into the saddle.

"You ever think that this whole thing might be a maneuver to run your people out of the valley?"

"I don't see what anybody would gain by that. There's a few hates us maybe, but I don't think as much as that."

"What about your land? It looks like the best in the valley to me."

"By and large, it is that. But the whole community gets the good of it. If we was to leave altogether, there'd be nobody to work it."

"It would bring a good price, wouldn't it?"

Mr. Asbury looked frightened. "I would think that is so. But Dr. Favra wouldn't do that. By and large, he's a fair man."

"What about Elwood Snowe?"

"He—well, he don't take to us much. But Dr. Favra runs things. He wouldn't allow no shenanigans."

They took a road eastward toward the range that rimmed the valley on that side. They crossed and recrossed the river on neat masonry bridges. Heat vapor shimmered above the wheat fields and the hillsides. Dust haze blunted distant contours. There was a sleepy softness to the air and Mayberly basked in dreamlike detachment. He had the feeling that the world had no more substance to it than a stereopticon picture projected upon smoke.

The road bent southward and he was startled out of his dreaminess by a view of the dam in the distance. Its tall masonry face rose majestically to seal a narrow canyon and dominate the valley below. It seemed a meaningful monument to the skill of man at making covenants with nature.

They halted at the turn in the road. Asbury pointed to a side road, hardly more than a wagon trace, that reached up the hillside to the east. The Johnson place was the other side of the rise, he said. When they neared the top, Mayberly left Asbury with the horses and walked ahead. He bend low as he neared the crest, left the road, and dropped to one knee to look down on the house below.

It was unpainted, raw-looking in the sun. It was almost at the bottom of the slope. There was a pile of lumber in the yard and a man and woman were working beside it. The man was sawing a board. The woman held the end of it to keep the cut from breaking prematurely. They had built the skelton of another building, probably a small barn. Mayberly flattened himself on his belly and studied other details of the scene. A creek sliced along the bottom of the slope with brush and grass along it. Two heavy horses and three light ones grazed here. The end of a covered wagon protruded from behind the house. It seemed probable that the Johnson family was the one that had camped on the river near Spinnerville. The family that Susanna Velasquez had joined.

As he watched, a boy came from behind the pile of lumber. He had an armful of scrap wood, and he crossed the yard and entered the house. The man completed his cut and laid another board across the sawhorses. The woman traded places with him then, taking the saw and beginning the new cut.

The boy came out of the house and stood by idly on the porch for a moment. A woman came into the doorway behind him and spoke to him. She said something that made him laugh. She must be Susanna Velasquez, Mayberly thought. But he could not see her clearly enough to be absolutely certain.

He slid back a little way, got to his feet, and returned to where Asbury was waiting with the horses. He pulled himself into the saddle and they swung back the way they had come.

They arrived at Asbury's "family" (a term that seemed to apply to the area as well as the people in it) too late for the evening meal and they ate a warmed-over supper in the kitchen. At the guesthouse, Mayberly found a cot made up for him with clean white sheets collared over gray blankets. He lay awake a long time, piecing out facts with guesswork, trying to find enough certainty to give him the basis for a plan.

There were no solid facts to indicate that Susanna had been in touch with the Ambrose brothers. She might simply have come up here and joined a family named Johnson. In a general way, Johnson fitted Sip's description and the boy was about the age of Sip's boy. But that wasn't enough. Where was Tucker? Who was the woman calling herself Mrs. Johnson?

To ask those two questions in that order was to suggest an answer that pulled Mayberly out of bed. He lighted a lamp, fumbled around in his clothing till he found a cigar. He sat on the bed puffing it, weighing the possibility that Tucker Ambrose had disguised himself in woman's clothing.

Scraps and bits of confirmation floated out of his memory in startling profusion. Tucker was small, almost dainty. And then there were the footprints Mayberly had tried to read back at the campsite south of Spinnerville. Susanna's had been easy to distinguish from the other woman's. It seemed to him that the latter had turned in a bit. He remembered now that Melody had said Tucker was pigeon-toed....

The little details were beginning to add up now. Mayberly decided that he could be fairly sure he had found the Ambrose brothers. And he could be dead sure before he made his final plans for taking them. He could see that Melody got a chance to identify Sip and the boy.

There was another aspect of the situation that needed sober appraisal. Elwood Snowe was here. Elwood's past connection with the Ambrose boys had been nebulous, uncertain. But it was unthinkable that his being here in New Sanity was mere coincidence. And then there was the dynamiting. That was either the work of a lone crackpot or it was part of a careful plan to discredit the Shakers. Elwood was a planner. So were Sip and Tucker Ambrose.... A remote, isolated communistic society was the last place anyone would be likely to look for a pair of notorious outlaws. Their being here was another demonstration of the craftiness with which they had avoided pursuit throughout their career. But to the idea of sanctuary add the idea of control of the colony. Then you had a plan that would be entirely in keeping with the characters of Elwood Snowe and of the Ambrose brothers as well.

Mayberly put out the cigar, blew the lamp, and went back to bed. He composed himself with the thought that

110

the people calling themselves the Johnsons had invested in a house and were building a barn. They meant to stay where they were for a long time. He had time to plan, to be sure of every step before he moved. . . .

He woke to a knocking on his door and found that Shakers rose before dawn. When he entered the dining hall for breakfast, his big Raymond watch read a quarter to five. When he had eaten and had had a brief talk with Asbury, he saddled up and rode back to Spinnerville.

At Mrs. Torgenson's boardinghouse, he found two sealed notes that had been shoved under his door. Both were from Melody.

The first said merely that Mr. Deeds had left on the northbound stage.

The second, terse though it was, conveyed a note of mild desperation:

> *Mr. D. came back to Spinnerville tonight. He went north only as far as Star City to send a telegram to the Pinkerton office in St. Paul. He asked them to send another man to Three Forks. He seems to feel that I, too, should be kept under surveillance and that he is the man for the job. Frankly, I doubt that your letter ever convinced him for more than a minute. That is probably my fault—I'm a rotten liar. What do I do now?*
>
> M.C.

At the courthouse, Mayberly found that the sheriff was out. Rather than go looking for him and risk being seen by Deeds, he decided to wait. He chatted with a deputy about trout flies and hunting rifles for the better part of an hour, evading the deputy's sly questions about his business with the sheriff. When the sheriff came in, he sent the deputy on an errand and eyed Mayberly expectantly.

Mayberly told him what there was to tell about the dynamiting of the colony guardhouse. He pointed out that any sort of violent action was out of keeping with the beliefs of the Shakers but that there seemed to be an irrational distrust of them on the part of the Patrol. The whole thing could be a plot to discredit the Shakers, he said. He didn't mention Elwood Snowe or the Johnson family.

"You don't win any prizes for sleuthing," the sheriff said. "But at least you were there and with a badge in your pocket. If something more serious develops, nobody can accuse the sheriff's office of turning its back."

"I'm going back out there," Mayberly said. "I mean to take Miss Coates with me. The problem will be to get her away from Deeds."

The sheriff eyed him with shrewd amusement. "If you're about to ask me to jail him for a couple of hours on some trumped-up charge, save your breath. I'm an ethical law officer, especially where Pinkertons are concerned. I suppose I might occupy his attention for a few minutes, long enough for you and your lady to sneak out of town. But it will have to wait. An hour ago Mr. Benjamin Deeds had the hotel pack a basket of food. He then rented a buggy and drove off with your lady. Looks like they're on a picnic."

Mayberrly cursed mightily. Melody had misled Deeds and she felt guilty about it. There was no telling what she might do or say on a picnic with the man.

"What you want to take her out to the colony for?" the sheriff asked.

"If I don't tell you, you won't have to lie to Deeds when he questions you."

"You found something out there. If the Ambrose boys

are in my county, I want to know it.''

"I'm not sure.''

The sheriff pushed back his chair and stared briefly at the ceiling. "When you're ready to make your move, I want to know it. To interfere with what Favra considers private colony business is one thing. To go out there after a couple of notorious criminals is another. He couldn't complain about that, and it would sort of straighten out this jurisdiction business. I want to be in on the kill, Mayberly.''

"I'm not splitting the reward. You understand that?''

"Don't worry about it. I never took a nickel of bounty money in my life. For that matter, I never heard of a Pinkerton man who did either. There's a company rule against it, I believe.''

"Just the same, we'll leave them out of this.''

The sheriff nodded. "They do have a way of moving in and taking over. Deeds will get no information out of me.''

"You got any handcuffs?''

"What for?''

"I'll bring you in on the kill if I can. God knows, I don't relish the idea of trying to take the Ambrose boys alone. I might try it if they should separate, though. Anyhow, I'd like a couple pair of handcuffs.''

"I've got three pairs of Beans and three Richardsons,'' the sheriff said, jerking open a drawer and clanking a maze of nickel-plated steel out of it to the desk top. "Take your choice.''

Mayberly selected two pairs. "Which way did they go?''

"Who?''

"Melody and Deeds.''

"South,'' the sheriff said. "Look here. You're packing

113

a deputy's badge. Don't you do anything to disgrace this office.''

The stages hadn't passed through Spinnerville yet this day and there had been little other traffic on the road, so Maberly found the buggy track easy enough to follow. A mile south of town it turned into an old mining road that wound up a hillside; but it was plain from the tracks that the buggy had returned to the stage road after a short side trip and that it had continued south. Deeds and Melody were in a mood for exploring, it seemed.

A few miles farther along, the river bend close to the road and then swung under a long bridge with a surface of worn planks. To the right, there was a little rise with pines scattered across it. The buggy tracks left the road here and curled up into the trees.

At the crest, Mayberly paused, glimpsing the buggy in a little meadow near the foot of the long slope below. The wind brought him the bright notes of a woman's laughter, and he had his moment of hesitation. Grimly, he urged his horse downward through the scattered pines.

After a few yards, he reined up abruptly. Off to the left, a saddle horse grazed among the pines. There was no sign of the rider. Mayberly rode over for a closer look at the horse. The saddle looked familiar. With a sinking feeling, he pulled the Winchester from the boot attached to the empty saddle. He knew at once that he had held the gun in his hands before.

11

HARRY YADKIN left Dancing D ranch soon after sunup. Since he was reasonably sure the Ambrose brothers had gone at least as far as Spinnerville, there was no need for him to ask about their wagon along the way. So he traveled at a fairly steady pace, nooned leisurely, and jogged into town late in the afternoon.

He stabled his horse, bought a new shirt, got a room at the hotel, and spent more than an hour washing up and trimming his mustache and beard. He went down to the hotel dining room for an early supper, intending to scout the town afterward for a small-stakes game suitable to his meager bankroll and limited talent. He was on his third cup of coffee and a slab of rhubarb pie when Melody Coates and Mr. Deeds came into the dining room.

Yadkin was completely surprised. They took a table not far from his with Melody choosing a chair that faced him. Deeds drew it out for her, and for an instant his eyes met Yadkin's. Yadkin was sure he had seen the man before, but he couldn't remember where or when. On the other hand, there was a fleeting, almost imperceptible reaction on Deed's part. A split second of hesitation, a stabbing glance, a too-quick turning of his back—these small things indicated to Yadkin that Deeds had probably recognized *him*.

He finished the pie and went out of the dining room and

across the balcony-ringed lobby to the bar. He put down a quick three fingers of whisky and lingered over a second. He returned to the lobby and slid a dollar of his poker stake across the registration desk to the clerk. A few minutes later he knew that the Coates woman had registered as Mrs. George Russell, that Deeds claimed to be connected with the Northern Pacific, that they had arrived on the same stage several days ago, that Deeds had left on the northbound stage today and had just returned, and that they had second-floor rooms that faced each other across the hollow center of the building. Telling the clerk that stair climbing was hard on a bad leg, he was allowed to move from the third floor down to the second. With his pocketknife he promptly bored a small hole in the upper panel of his door so he could watch both of theirs.

The next morning when Deeds rented a buggy and swung up the street to pick up Melody, Yadkin was already on his way down an alley toward the livery. He saddled his horse, watched from the dark interior of the barn as the buggy rolled south out of town. In a few moments he followed.

He gave them a lead of a full mile, which meant that in this rolling country they were out of sight a good part of the time. When they turned off on a mining road, he traveled cross-country and watched from a distance while the buggy climbed a hillside to an old shaft, circled, and started back. It seemed to him at this point that Deeds and the woman were searching for something, and he began to feel hopeful excitement. Later, they left the stage road again and wove over a pine-dappled hill. Following to its top, he watched them halt on the slope below and take a covered basket from the buggy. He realized then that they were probably just on a pleasure jaunt.

His dissapointment was sharp. Still, considering the place they had chosen, his day might not be completely wasted. He might get close enough to eavesdrop. They might say something revealing.

They had chosen a small, tree-fringed meadow for their picnic. Melody spread a tablecloth on the grass near a rock outcropping. They both sat down and she began to lay out food from the basket. The perpendicular face of the outcropping rose eight or ten feet above them. Its opposite side, however, was hummock-like. Brush and pine seedlings grew out of the earth and erosion there.

Yadkin swung his horse off to the left where there was some browse. He left the animal here and made his way down through the pines on foot. He circled the meadow to put the outcropping between him and the picnickers. He climbed silently through the scattered brush to the crest. Then he lay on his belly and worked to a position where he could look down on the man and woman and hear almost every word they said.

They were munching sandwiches. As far as Yadkin was concerned, their talk was silly courting talk, at least at first. Deeds couldn't take his eyes off the woman. It was plain he had a bad case of petticoat fever. It seemed as if there was nothing else on his mind. Maybe he wasn't a Pinkerton after all, Yadkin thought.

"Stop it Ben," Melody said. "I'm trying to eat."

"You think of the silliest reasons for discouraging me," Deeds said.

"Besides, I'm a well-bred girl who doesn't spoon with strange men."

"Strange men! Melody—"

"Did you try a chicken sandwich?"

"Melody, is there someone else?"

117

"Hush. Eat your lunch."

"Please, answer the question."

"I've told you there isn't," she said. "In Castle Rock, men stayed away from me in droves. Nobody wants to be known as your man friend when you're raising an outlaw's son. Besides, I guess I'm sort of standoffish about men. I don't mean to be, but I can't help it. I saw my older sister do an impulsive, headstrong thing. I saw her after her life had been turned into hell on earth and I saw her die. That did something to me, I guess."

"Haven't you ever felt that you need somebody?"

"Of course I have. Are there any more of those pickles?"

"But you don't need me?"

"Right now I need to find Stevie. I can't trust my feelings about anything else until I do."

"But there's nobody else?"

Melody sighed noisily. "How many times do I have to say it?"

Then Deeds said something that made Yadkin pick up his ears.

"What about Mayberly?"

"What about him?" Melody said.

"Are you fond of him?"

"You're being just plain ridiculous, Ben. I've talked to the man twice in my life. He's very attractive in some ways. But he's a bounty hunter and I'm sure—"

"Wait a minute," Deeds said. "The last I knew, you'd seen him once in your life, not twice."

"Well, once then."

"I think you just trapped yourself. He isn't in Three Forks, is he? You've seen him since we arrived here, haven't you?"

"I'm not going to discuss my business with Mr. Mayberly."

"Now whoa up," Deeds said. "You weren't the least bit hesitant about discussing that letter with me. It was a fake, wasn't it? It was supposed to get me out of here, wasn't it? And Mayberly is right here around Spinnerville somewhere."

"Ben, you're interrogating me. I want some more lemonade."

Deeds got to his feet to get the jar of lemonade that had been carefully set aside in the shade of a rock. Yadkin cautiously slid back a couple of feet, cussing mentally.

Mayberly here! It was plain that he and the Coates woman were working together, after all. The argument they had back in Laramie must have been staged. Now the Pinkerton was courting her and trying to find out where Mayberly was and what he was on to. Maybe the Pinkerton wasn't quite so much of a fool as he looked. Yadkin felt a certain sympathy for him.

He began to ease back through the brush. He decided now that it must have been at Laramie that he had seen Deeds. Deeds had recognized him last night in the dining room—that was almost certain. There was nothing further to be gained from this kind of snooping. It was time to talk deal.

He got down from the outcropping and into the cover of the pines. Moving silently, he skirted the meadow and strode into it from the other side. He gave a little wave of his hand as he approached the picnickers.

"Been trailing you folks all the way from town. Want to have a talk with you."

Deeds gestured wearily with a half-eaten sandwich.

"Mr. Yadkin."

"How do you do?" Melody said.

Yadkin nodded at her. He sat down and embraced his knees. It seemed to him that they might offer him a sandwich and some lemonade, but they didn't.

"You're a detective," he said to Deeds. "I know some information about the Ambrose boys that you don't. We might make a trade, looks like. Maybe we might work together. They ain't going to be easy to take, the Ambroses."

"Only if you know something mighty important," Deeds said.

"I don't know where they're at right exact so you could spit on the place. But I know they come through here a few days back."

"Came through?"

"Come through or holed up, I won't say for certain. But I will say this. Unless you know what I know, you won't be likely to find 'em."

"And what is that?"

"This is where we come to the trading part."

"The fact is," Deeds said, "that I hardly think we have anything to trade with."

"I'd like to know first off what brought you to this part of the country."

Deeds made a cynical little gesture with his sandwich. "Mayberly."

"You followed him here?"

"He told Melody to come here and wait. I followed her. He sent her word that he had gone to Three Forks, but I suspect that was a deception." Deeds turned to Melody, staring narrowly at her. She avoided his eyes at first and then met them defiantly.

"And you don't know no more'n that?" Yadkin said.

"I suspect Miss Coates does."

Yadkin gave Melody a long, patient look and then turned back to Deeds. "She is a foolish woman if she puts any trust in Mayberly. He is no better'n an outlaw himself. Down near Laramie, he held me up and robbed me of every cent I had in my jeans."

"I don't believe that," Melody said.

"I swear to Jesus. He robbed me and set me afoot."

"You were following him, spying on him."

"Yes, ma'am, I was. He wouldn't talk deal, so I trailed him. He's crazy, ma'am. He thinks the Ambroses are his own private property. I say that's crazy. He is not a trustworthy person. I remember once down to Stonewall—"

Neither Melody nor Deeds were paying attention. Both were staring past Yadkin. He turned and saw that a rider had come out of the pines and into the meadow.

Yadkin leaped to his feet. He stood with his right elbow bent, his fingers touching the handle of his revolver. Mayberly reined up five yards away, swinging his horse so its right side was toward the group. He shifted slightly in the saddle.

"Pull that gun, Harry, and I'll kill you where you stand. You know that."

Yadkin moved his hand away from the gun. Mayberly got down from his horse, dropping the reins. He walked straight up to Yadkin and removed the gun from the man's holster. He then stooped and lifted the derringer from inside the little holster inside his right boot. He faced Deeds, who got to his feet.

"You'll be wearing a shoulder holster." Mayberly opened Deeds's coat and extracted a small revolver from

121

under his left armpit.

"What do you want?" Deeds demanded.

"I told you—" Yadkin said. "He is no better'n an outlaw. He will rob us and set us afoot."

Mayberly ejected the bullets from the guns and threw the weapons over the outcropping. He then went to his horse, removed a pair of handcuffs from the saddlebags, and turned back toward Deeds.

Deeds took one look at the handcuffs and moved swiftly and expertly. He aimed two fingers of his left hand at Mayberly's right eye, missing by a scant inch, and then brought up his right fist in a short uppercut that caught Mayberly on the side of the jaw and staggered him backward. Yadkin now went into action, throwing a shoulder into Mayberly's midsection while he was off balance and grabbing for the revolver at Mayberly's hip.

Mayberly went down. As he fell, he brought the handcuffs down in a clubbing motion precisely, almost gently behind Yadkin's ear. Yadkin fell in front of him, between him and Deeds, who leaped toward Mayberly and aimed a kick that missed as the big man rolled. Deeds took a long step and kicked again, but Mayberly had his feet under him by that time and caught the foot with crossed hands, twisted it, and sent Deeds sprawling. He caught Deeds by the arm and pulled him to his feet, locking a section of the handcuffs to his wrist as he did so.

Yadkin sat up, looking dazed and feeling his head. Mayberly swung Deeds around and tripped him so he fell into Yadkin. He then stooped and seized Yadkin's right foot. Putting his own foot into Yadkin's crotch, he wrenched off the boot.

Deeds, quickly on his feet, gripped the handcuffs so as to make a weapon of them and rushed toward Mayberly.

Mayberly flung Yadkin's boot at Deeds's head, boring in close behind it and catching Deeds's arm as Deeds dodged. He quickly got an armlock, bent the arm behind Deeds's back, and tripped him so he fell beside Yadkin with Mayberly on top of him. Mayberly then snapped the free side of the handcuffs around Yadkin's ankle.

He got up, retrieved his hat, dusted himself off. Melody gaped at the two men on the ground and then at Mayberly. He picked up the picnic basket, added the jar of lemonade to it, and started toward the buggy. This, along with the tie iron, had been dragged to the edge of the meadow by the grazing horse.

"Come on," he said over his shoulder to Melody. "You're coming with me."

"I most certainly am not." She found herself speaking to his back. "Do you think you can ride in here and behave like a—a beast and—and order me around and I'll jump?"

He swung the basket into the boot behind the buggy seat. He unsnapped the tie iron and put that in beside the basket. Catching a rein near the horse's head, he swung the buggy around and across the meadow toward Melody.

"Get in," he said. "It's important."

Melody retreated a step toward the men on the ground. They were helplessly examining the handcuffs that bound them together, wrist to ankle. Yadkin began to cuss shamelessly.

"Don't go with him," Deeds said to Melody. "Make him force you. We'll add a kidnaping charge to the list we already have against him. He'll learn you don't attack a Pinkerton man and not pay for it."

"Ben," she said, "it looked to me as if *you* attacked *him*."

Mayberly had to laugh at that. "Come to think of it,

Deeds, you did. It looks like I've got a witness too. Get into the buggy, Melody.''

''You said—it's important?''

''I think so.''

''What about them? You're not going to leave them here— fastened together like that?''

''They'll make it to the road eventually, although Deeds will probably have to carry Yadkin. If they're lucky, some farmer will come along in a wagon and give them a lift.''

She glared at him, then turned to Deeds and said apologetically, ''I have to do what's best for Stevie.''

She quickly got into the buggy. Following Mayberly's instructions, she took the reins and followed him out of the meadow and over the hill toward the road. Near the summit, he caught up the reins of Yadkin's horse and took it along.

They turned north into the road. After a mile and a half, Mayberly called a halt.

''We'll leave the buggy here. The horse will take it back to the livery, I should think. Can you ride astride?''

She gave him the hint of a smile. ''I grew up on a farm. But why? Where are we going?''

''Get on Yadkin's horse then. We're going to the colony, the place called New Sanity. The sensible thing would be to ride through town and take the road just the other side of it. But we're going cross-country, first east and then north. The idea is to throw your friends off our track. They'll discover that the horse returned without us. By the time they do, there will have been enough traffic so they won't be likely to figure out where we left the road. They'll know only that it was somewhere south of town, which should suggest we are *not* going to the colony.''

"Whatever you say. Do you mind telling me why we're going there?"

"Don't get your hopes up, Melody. I'm not completely certain, but I think I've found your nephew."

He got down and got the picnic basket from the buggy, then started the horse for town. He gave Melody a leg up, mounted his own horse again, and led the way with the basket hooked over his arm.

They worked into the hills to the east till they came to a stream that he knew must be Singing River. They followed it northward to the reservoir and took a narrow trail along the steep east bank to the dam.

High and lonely between rock-faced buttes, the dam shouldered back blue water that turned green as it slipped over a spillway. Below, the valley rolled out, green and golden, laced with irrigation ditches and checkered with fenced pastures and fields of yellowing wheat. The wide-beached line of the river channel bent westward to the cluster of rooftops that was New Sanity headquarters; then it looped on northward into the widening wedge of farmland that hazed away into blue mountains at its distant rim. There was the feel of time as well as space in the view, of home and hope and brother banding, of men who believed and toiled, of earth's response.

They halted beside the dam and had their silent look. Then Mayberly pointed off to the right where a little side valley curled out between low hills. It was an old channel, probably, a flood course of the days before the dam. The first quarter mile was barren, rocky, then a creek creased down to green it. Beyond, before the valley curved away, new lumber scarred its western slope. A house stood there and the skeleton of a barn.

"That's the Johnson place," Mayberly said. "I came

125

on it yesterday from the west, but there's a road on that side and a chance of being seen. We'll circle that hill to the east and try to get into the brush near its top. I've got field glasses in my saddlebags.''

"You think Stevie's there?''

"There was a boy in the yard yesterday.''

A man had come out of the cabin on the far side of the reservoir and was watching them. He waved uncertainly and moved toward the dam as if to cross it. Mayberly returned his greeting and reined away.

Ten minutes later they left the horses in a grassy pocket and made their way around the curve of the hill to the brush he had pointed out. Most of it was knee-high stuff with a few scraggly junipers rising out of it. Mayberly led the way into it, bending low, and they crawled on hands and knees the last few yards to a flat, relatively barren bulge in the hillside. Here they lay on their stomachs and looked down across the creek to the Johnson place.

There were no horses grazing on the slope above the creek and the wagon was gone. Yet there was a plume of smoke rising from the chimney as if someone had just started a fire in the kitchen stove.

"They aren't all there,'' Mayberly said.

The day was wearing away; there would be not much more than an hour of strong light left. He had brought along the field glasses from his saddlebags as well as the lunch basket. He passed the glasses to Melody.

"Focus on the yard beside the porch.''

While she was doing this, he dug into the basket for a sandwich and bit into it hungrily. She gave him a glance and went back to her focusing.

"Lucky there's some lunch left,'' he said. "We may be here all night.''

"I hope you're joking," she said.

"I'm not. We can move around the hill near the horses after dark. I've got two blankets in my saddlebags."

"That won't do, Mr. Mayberly. You'll have to think of something better."

The missing horses and wagon puzzled him. Why were the saddle horses gone as well as the team? Possible explanations nagged at him, made him edgy. His mood got worse as the sun set and the light thickened. They were both uncomfortable. Melody kept changing her position. They ate the rest of the sandwiches and washed them down with warm lemonade. When a light shone in a window of the house, they gave up.

"I know," Melody said as she followed him around the hill toward the horses, "If I hadn't gone on that picnic, we could have been here hours earlier. Maybe we would have seen something."

Mayberly turned to give her a rare smile. "If you hadn't gone on the picnic, I'd have found a way to sneak you away from Deeds, but I didn't know Yadkin was here. He'd have followed us. The picnic was a lucky thing."

"Then you're not angry?"

"No."

"Sometimes, Mr. Mayberly, you seem angry at the world."

"Right now I'm worried about that missing wagon. If it isn't back by morning, I may go looking for it. I may leave you up there with the glasses alone."

"And we're going to spend the night here?"

"You said that wouldn't do."

"Where are we going?"

"I'm taking you to the north end of the valley, to a Shaker community. It's a considerable ride, but you'll have privacy and a proper bed. We'll get up before daylight and come back here.''

For a moment she stopped dead still, surprised that he thought of an alternative to their spending the night together under the stars. She was even (and Melody Coates admitted it to herself with a mental shudder) a little bit disappointed.

12

PA HAD drawn a map and had gone over the plan gosh knew how many times. He had gone over it twice with Mr. Snowe and again and again with Uncle Tucker. Stevie knew every detail by heart, just from hearing it so often.

The important thing was to get the timing right. They were going to have a real early supper, and Pa and Uncle Tucker were going into Spinnerville. They were going to take the wagon and the saddle horses. If anybody got curious about it, their reason was that they were going to ask around about a buyer for the saddle horses.

It would be after dark when they started back, not having made a deal. Uncle Tucker would pull the wagon off the road after they got out of town. The box of dynamite would be in the wagon. Pa would take it and ride on ahead. Uncle Tucker would wait one hour and ten minutes before he followed.

When Pa reached New Sanity, he would turn north at the crossroads at the edge of the headquarters area. He would ride north all the way to the first Shaker settlement. The Shakers never went anywhere at night except to meeting, so he wasn't likely to meet anybody on the road. At the settlement he would turn around. He would ride back to the phalanstery. He would consult his watch and get there five minutes after ten. He would plant the dynamite in the cellar of the phalanstery. There was an outside entrance to the cellar that Mr. Snowe guaranteed would be unlocked.

Pa would use all the rest of the dynamite in the box. He would place it so as to demolish the north end of the building. Dr. Favra's bedroom was at the south end and he went to bed at exactly ten o'clock. They didn't want to kill Dr. Favra yet. They wanted to get him mad at the Shakers first. They wanted him to denounce them publicly, as Mr. Snowe put it. Then they would kill him and the Shakers would be blamed. They didn't seem to care if other people should happen to get killed. Mr. Snowe was going to be attending a meeting of the Philosophical Society in another building.

There would be a five-minute fuse on the dynamite. That would give Pa time to get past the crossroads, headed toward town. He would meet Uncle Tucker, who would also be checking his watch, just the other side of the crossroads. Pa would throw his saddle into the wagon and tie his horse on behind with the others. They would be almost to the crossroads when the blast went off.

They would drive on up to the phalanstery and join the crowd that would gather. Uncle Tucker would be dressed as a woman, of course, and he would not get out of the wagon. If anyone spoke to him, he was just to shake his head stunned-like and not to talk if he could avoid it. After a bit, Pa would say his woman was sick and they would drive home.

The important thing was that the wagon and the trailing horses would obliterate the tracks that Pa had left on the town road. There would be only the two sets of recent tracks he left on the crossroad on his ride to the Shaker colony and back. The Patrol would naturally assume that

130

it was the other way around, that the rider had started out at the Shaker colony. It would look as if he had come to the phalanstery, set off the explosion, and then ridden back the way he had come.

There were a lot of fine points to the plan. For instance, when Pa first reached the crossroads, coming from town, he would ride past it a few yards. Then he would turn around and cut the corner into it at a gallop. Pa went over the details so often that Uncle Tucker got tired of listening.

"My God, Sip," he said. "I got it all in my head just as clear as you have. Stop talking to me like I'm slow-minded."

"Sometimes you act like it," Pa snapped.

"I ain't exactly feeling up to snuff. You know that. But I ain't a slooney, neither. One good jolt of good whisky—"

"You never took one jolt in your life."

"The hell I never. Sip, it ain't as if I wanted it right now. I won't touch a drop till this is over."

"Not for a while yet, Tuck."

"When?"

"When Favra's out of the way."

"When will that be?"

"When Elwood says so. Not long. Maybe a few days."

"Sip, I didn't come off that last binge right. I still got biliousness and the nervous flutters."

"That ain't surprisin', the amount you put away."

"Seems like after this job we could have a couple drinks together. You could pick up a bottle in town. One bottle."

"Goddamn it, no."

"A pint."

"Tuck," Pa said. "I'm puttin' my foot down on this. I don't want to hear no more argufyin' about it."

Uncle Tucker fell silent. After a moment, Pa said, "When Elwood takes over, we'll go on a toot then, Tuck. The both of us."

Stevie helped Pa catch the horses and hitch the team. Pa stowed the dynamite and his saddle in the back of the wagon. Aunt Sue had Uncle Tucker all prettied up. She had arranged the switch of false hair so it showed at the sides of the poke bonnet. He looked more like a dowdy farm wife than ever.

Stevie watched them drive off with a mixture of feelings that left him dull and confused. He still wanted to get back to Aunt Melody. He wanted that more than anything. But he had come to think of it as a someday thing. Not a thing that could happen soon. He hated the ugliness of what Pa and Uncle Tucker were going to do, but he didn't want anything to go wrong either. He was fond of Uncle Tucker and he had sort of got used to Pa. He just wished Pa didn't hate everybody so much.

Being left alone with Aunt Sue, he supposed he might make a run for it, but that would be just plain foolish. There was no place to go. Pa and Uncle Tucker would be in town; he wouldn't dare go there. And Elwood Snowe was at New Sanity headquarters. Heading off into the wilderness would be pointless. Pa would trail him and find him quick enough. He didn't like to think about what Pa would do when he caught him.

Besides, he liked being with Aunt Sue. She was full of fun and interested in things and easy to talk to. She seemed to understand that he meant to get away someday. Sometimes she hinted that she might help him.

When Pa and Uncle Tucker were working on the barn,

she spent a lot of time poking around the house, looking for money. Sometimes she would ask Stevie to help with the housework. Then he would come in and keep a look-out at a window and warn her if one of the men started for the house.

There was a bag of gold and silver coins, most of it done up in rolls, under the bed. She found that right off. She said there was only a little more than a thousand dollars there and that there was a lot more around somewhere. It was in paper money, she said. Big bills of a hundred dollars or even bigger that would be hard to pass without arousing suspicion. They would be in a small package, she said, maybe not much bigger than a brick.

Stevie had asked her what she would do if she found it. "Pa would kill you if you ran off, wouldn't he?"

"If I ever run off, I'll go so fast and so far he'll never find me," she said. She added, "Would you like to go with me?"

He replied guardedly and she mussed his hair the way she was always doing and that was the end of it. But he was left with a new hope.

Now, as soon as the wagon was out of sight over the hill, she began searching the house again. She looked in the loft and the closets and under the mattresses and in a dozen other places, some of which she had looked in before. Then she went out on the porch and looked through some gear that was stowed there—Uncle Tucker's saddle and saddlebags and rifle and boots and some canteens and a knapsack.

One of the canteens was gallon size, shaped like a store cheese or a hugh birthday cake. She picked it up, shook it, felt a small lump under the dirty canvas covering. She laid the canteen aside, then suddenly picked it up again. She unsnapped the covering and slipped it off.

There was a seam about two-thirds of the way down on the metal container. It ran all the way around. She pushed hard on one edge of the lower section and it began to slide out. It seemed that there was a false bottom in the top part so it would hold water. Flanges had been soldered under it and also to the lower section so the two parts would fit together tightly but could be slid apart.

Aunt Sue took one quick look into the lower section and shoved it back flush again. She fitted the tight canvas cover back onto the canteen again and put the rest of the gear back just as it had been. She went into the house and dropped into a chair beside the kitchen table. She looked kind of dazed. All at once she turned to Stevie.

"You know better than to breathe a word of this." There was a hardness in her voice that was new to him.

"Yes, ma'am."

"If you do—well, never mind."

"Are you going away now?" he asked.

"Never mind about that."

"I think I'd like to go with you."

She smiled and her manner softened a little. "I don't know. Your father has got into something that is new to him. He's just lucky enough so that maybe it will work. Maybe if we stick it out, we'll both be rich, really rich. But I don't know. I don't like that Mr. Snowe, and the whole thing seems a little crazy to me."

After a while she got up and stirred up the fire and took a cloth off a bowl of dough that had been set to rise. She went about baking bread just as if nothing had changed. She kept looking at the small gold watch that she sometimes wore pinned to her dress. It was on the table now, and Stevie kept watching it too.

When the bread was done, they ate some of it with pale sweet butter that came from the New Sanity creamery. A man from the creamery called every other day. He asked what you needed and gave it to you and you didn't have to pay for it. After a while Aunt Sue got a pack of cards and they played cassino to pass the time.

Ten o'clock came and five minutes after. Pa would be at the phalanstery, placing the dynamite. Stevie felt excited and sort of sick to his stomach. They played another hand and then just waited. A quarter after ten came. Sixteen after. Then the explosion came. It was loud and sharp. It rattled the windows, and the lamp flickered briefly. The echo rumbled in the hills and then there was silence.

Stevie met Aunt Sue's eyes and saw that she was as scared as he was. There were dark lines in her face and for a moment she looked like an old woman. She smiled then and said, "Hallelujah. They'll be here in a few minutes. You better get to bed."

She sounded as if she didn't really care and he didn't move. He picked up the pack of cards and stared at it, pouring his attention into the small intricacies of the back design. Aunt Sue reached over and took the cards from him and dealt another hand.

Eleven o'clock came. Pa and Uncle Tucker were not back. Aunt Sue made frequent trips to the window now to watch for them. She would stay at the window a short time and then come back to the table and they would play another hand. Eleven- thirty. They both knew something had gone wrong but neither mentioned it. Aunt Sue didn't say anything more about going to bed.

It was after midnight when there was the sound of hoofs in the yard. Aunt Sue slapped down her cards and rushed to the window and then to the door. She opened it and Pa stomped in. He looked flushed and wild-eyed.

"You ain't seen or heard nothing of Tucker?"

"No," Aunt Sue said. "What—"

"He's lost," Pa said. "I left him pulled off the road like we planned. He was supposed to meet me near the crossroads. He wasn't there. He wasn't no place on the road. Damned if I know where to look."

13

TUCKER AMBROSE sat on the wagon seat and rolled a cigarette and smoked it. They had been to town and asked about horse buyers and had started back. They had pulled the wagon into a little gully out of sight of the road. Sip had gone on ahead on horseback to lay the false trail down to the Shaker colony and back.

It was that dreary time of evening when darkness is not quite complete. There was no stirring of air and the day's heat hung trapped in the gully, in the covered wagon, in the woman's clothing that Tucker wore. He consulted his watch, holding it at arm's length and tipping it to catch the last thin light.

Eight thirty-two. An hour to sit and wait. Well, he guessed he was going to do it. It was only a ten-minute drive back to town and would make the time pass faster. He would buy just a pint. He would drink none of it till this job was finished and they were back at the house. Absolutly none of it. He'd resisted the stuff before. Down in Colorado, he and Sip had traveled for a week once with a quart of tequila in his saddlebags. They'd hit the bank at Oak Springs and got to that hideout cabin near Dos Pinos before they had their first drink.

He clucked at the horses and swung the wagon out of the gully and into the road. He kept them at a trot most of the way, slowing them as he entered town. He took his purse from the pocket of his dress and took a five-dollar gold piece from it. He halted the team in front of the saloon and waited. He didn't dare go into the saloon. A woman in a saloon would attract altogether too much scrutiny. When a young man came along the boardwalk, Tucker called to him.

"Sir!"

The young man halted, touched his hat. He had a sort of lean look and was probably a cowhand down on his luck. Tucker beckoned him closer and remembered to keep his voice soft and ladylike.

"I want to ask a favor. My husband is down with the whooping croup and the doctor said to give him whiskey and honey. I'm embarrassed to go into the saloon. You suppose you'd buy a bottle of whisky for me?"

"Sure." The young man accepted the gold piece, glancing at it with something like awe. "You want a pint?"

"You better get a quart."

"Yes, ma'am. What kind of whisky? Red-eye is a dollar and a quarter a quart. Genuine Kentucky whisky is a dollar six bits."

"Kentucky. Make that two quarts of Kentucky whisky."

The young man gave Tucker a sharp look. "That must be some croup your husband's got."

"It is. Have the barkeep pull the cork on one of the bottles."

The young man went into the saloon. He returned promptly with two quarts of whisky and a dollar and a half in change. Tucker gave him the fifty cents for his trouble.

"I wouldn't accept it, ma'am, except—well, I'm down on my uppers for sure."

"Don't you spend it on a drink now," Tucker said.

He fished the watch out of the pocket of his dress and looked at it by the light of the town's one street lamp as he passed the courthouse. Eleven minutes to eight. There was still going to be a long wait in that damned gully. What the hell, he thought. All I have to do is drive the wagon. He worked the loosened cork out of a bottle and took a long smell and a sizable drink.

The whisky was scalding. He gasped noisily as its heat bit into his stomach. When it had faded to a gentle, spreading warmth, he tipped the bottle again. Then he put the cork back into it and put it under the seat.

Easy, he told himself. Take it easy, Tuck. You are in the middle of a job. You never drank on a job before. You got to drink sensible. You can do it. A few nips will steady you down, but take it easy. Then he cursed aloud.

"I believe that son of a bitch brought me red-eye!"

He picked up the bottle but couldn't see the label clearly in the darkness. He pulled the cork and took another drink. It tasted smoother this time, but he still wasn't sure it was genuine Kentucky. He took a long drink and decided that it was. Smooth, proper-aged Kentucky whisky that would treat a mind kindly....

He turned into the gully. The wagon hit a rock and almost pitched him off the seat. He reined up and had another drink and a look around. He was, he decided, in the wrong gully. He must have passed the other one. He tried to turn the wagon around and almost turned it over. He then unhitched the trailing saddle horses and backed the wagon onto the road. He headed back toward town. It didn't matter much of a whoop what gully he waited in, he supposed, except that it was related to the timing Sip had worked out. He couldn't find the first gully. He couldn't even find a place to turn around till he was almost to town.

He made the turn, wishing he could go back to that saloon and go in and kick up his heels a bit. If it wasn't for these fool clothes, damn it, he'd do it. A man needed a little sociability.

It was getting to be one hell of a dark night. There would be no moon till after midnight; Sip had figured on that. Tucker guessed it had clouded up too. He couldn't find the damn gully. He overtook a couple of loose horses on the road. After he had passed them, it came to him that they were his; he had forgotten to tie them on after he backed out of the rocky gully. It took a few minutes to catch them, then he had a couple more draws at the bottle. He got out his watch but couldn't read it in the darkness. He had tucked a handful of matches into his padded bosom but now he couldn't find one. He stood up and wiggled in the hope that one would sift down through his clothing, but that didn't work. He gave up on trying to read the watch and had a drink and headed on toward New Sanity.

He figured he had plenty of time and he drove slowly, stopping now and then to try to read the watch and to pull at the giant killer. He still couldn't decide whether it was red-eye or Kentucky. He reached the crossroads near the phalanstery and pulled up. He must be early, he thought. The only thing to do was turn around, go back a little way, turn around again, and take another shot at it.

He was right at the intersection. The horses were eager to get home and balky about turning. During the maneuver, the whisky bottle fell off the seat beside him to the floor of the wagon. He bent to recover it, afraid he hadn't put the cork back in or that it might have broken. The horses, still bent on home, continued the turn, making a full circle.

140

Tucker recovered the bottle, corked and unbroken. He grasped what had happened, cussed the horses, and pulled hard on the left rein to take them around toward town again. The bottle fell and rolled across the seat and he grabbed it and put it between his feet. The horses wanted to keep on going on around but he got them straightened out and on their way down the road. He had a good hard pull at the bottle and was surprised by how light it felt. He rejected the possibilty that he had drunk most of a quart of whisky in the short time since he left town. He must have spilled some of it, he concluded.

He didn't notice that he was passing the phalanstery on his right when it should have been behind him and that he had taken the north road instead of the road to town.

He corked the bottle and put it back between his feet. Easy, he reminded himself. Take it easy, Tucker. He ought to make another try at reading his watch, but it wasn't in his pocket and he couldn't find it. He would just have to guess at the timing. He would watch for a place to turn around in— No, he had already turned around. Back there where the horses had given him a bad time. All he had to do was sit on the wagon seat and look sober when Sip rode up. . . .

He was a quarter mile past the phalanstery when the dynamite went off. The explosion shocked him into a fleeting sense of something wrong. But it also frightened the horses, who leaped into a gallop, and his attention was instantly claimed by the need to stop a runaway. He undertook this with great calmness, determined to keep the bottle upright between his feet. In time, he managed it. He rewarded himself with a drink. All he had to do was sit on the wagon seat, and he was content. It never entered his mind that he had reached the crossroads when Sip was entering the phalanstery cellar to place the dynamite. Or that he was on the wrong road, headed the wrong way, and erasing the false trail that Sip had so carefully laid.

The meetinghouse of the first Shaker "family" was lighted, but it was half a mile off the main road and Tucker didn't notice it. He had knocked the neck off the second quart and was singing a ribald lullaby to the horses when, considerably later, he reached the Asbury "family."

The meetinghouse here was lighted too. It was only a few yards off the road and there was noise coming from open windows. Tucker reined up. He straightened the poke bonnet and make a careful descent from the wagon, beaming with sociability.

14

THEY GOT to their feet as best they could. Deeds worked the handcuffs as high as possible up Yadkin's shin. Deeds couldn't stand erect, of course, because of the other part of the cuffs locked on his wrist. He faced Yadkin, and Yadkin bent over his shoulder. Now Deeds straightened, lifting Yadkin in what is known as the fireman's carry.

Deeds started off up the hill. Because of the handcuffs, it was hard to get the balance right and he couldn't go far without a rest. He had to rest five times before they got over the hill to the road.

He was a strong man, stronger than he looked. He also had enough sense not to wear himself out. They began the trip up the road in legs of a hundred paces with rests in between. Deeds counted stolidly. Yadkin, head down over his shoulder, grunted the same tired obscenities over and over again, all aimed at Mayberly.

After half an hour and a quarter of a mile, they got lucky. A man in a buggy overtook them and halted. He turned out to be the Spinnerville doctor returning from a country call. He was understandably suspicious of two disheveled and sweat-streaked men handcuffed together. When he heard that they wanted to be taken directly to the sheriff, he gave them a ride.

He parked the buggy in front of the courthouse and went in and got the sheriff, who came out and unlocked the cuffs. Deeds demanded to know if Mayberly was in town. The sheriff said he didn't think so. He mentioned that the horse had brought the empty buggy back to the livery.

Deeds, stolid until now, let his anger out in a torrent of threats and demands. He reminded the sheriff that the Pinkerton organization would look after its own. He wanted Mayberly jailed. He wanted to know how come those were county handcuffs he and Yadkin had been sharing. Yadkin interrupted him.

"Damn it to hell, you should have done your cussing along the road like I did. Now you're wasting time. Me, I'm going to rent a horse and go back and find where Mayberly and that girl went. He probably brushed away their tracks where they left the road, but they won't be hard to pick up if I can find where the buggy stopped. You want to come along?"

Deeds regarded him wearily. "I guess I do."

Yadkin led him away from the sheriff. "We'll need a couple canteens and a couple rifles. Maybe some hardtack and jerky too. You rustle them up while I get the horses."

Traffic had chewed up the road since the buggy had returned, but Yadkin was a shrewd tracker. By concentrating on the edges of the road, he found a woman's footprint and, after scouting around a bit, announced that this was where the buggy had stopped. Mayberly had made a hurried effort to sweep the tracks near the road. But in a few minutes Deeds and Yadkin were following the trail left by his and Melody's horses.

Darkness was falling by the time they reached Singing River. Once he determined that Mayberly had crossed the stream and turned north, Yadkin stopped looking for tracks and they merely followed the stream. They reached the lake, black and silent, and picked their way along the trail on its steep bank. They reached the dam and halted. Yadkin pointed to a lighted window in a cabin on the other side of the reservoir. He got down from his horse, and Deeds watched him walk across the top of the dam.

The cabin door opened with Yadkin's lean hunched figure silhouetted in its doorway. He talked a long time with the man inside. Then the door closed and Yadkin came back across the dam.

He came close to Deeds's horse and laid a hand on its withers. His face was tense, his nose white and knife-thin above the darkness of his beard. Excitement honed a shrill note into his voice.

"They was here. Moved on before the damkeeper could talk to 'em. He seen 'em go around the east side of that hill there. Then they come around the hill on foot. The damkeeper put a telescope on 'em. Mayberly had that picnic basket on his arm. They went into some brush high up on the hill. They stayed till dark and the damkeeper couldn't see 'em no more. They're still there for all he knows."

Deeds scowled down on the dark valley. "Mayberly could be playing the lover. Maybe that's all he wanted."

"They didn't do no spoonin', the damkeeper said. And they had a pair of field glasses. See the light down there? That comes from a new-built house. Belongs to a family called Johnson. They arrived a few days ago in a covered wagon. Mayberly and the girl was watching that house."

Mayberly and Melody rode north alone the east bank of the river, traveling as fast as darkness and an unfamiliar trail would permit. They crossed a bridge about a mile above the Asbury "family." They had made the crossing and turned into the northbound wagon road when the explosion rolled the valley.

At this distance its sharpness was blunted. It reached them as a sudden rumbling, echoed dimly and then gone. Melody took it for a clap of thunder. She threw Mayberly a look and said idly, "Thank heaven we'll have a roof over our heads."

Mayberly knew at once that the sound was not thunder. He concealed his alarm and rode on in silence. The explosion came from the south, the general direction of New Sanity headquarters. He weighed the meaning of a new act of destruction there.

They reached the Asbury buildings and found most of them dark or showing only the pallid glimmer of turned-down lamps. Only the meetinghouse was brightly lighted. From it came the sound of chanting voices.

He took Melody to the guesthouse and they dismounted. He was still carrying the picnic basket, which he handed to her while he got his saddlebags and blanket roll. He would shed these, he thought. He wanted to travel fast and light.

He took the gear into the men's section and lighted a lamp. His cot had been made up for him and its prim pattern stabbed him with a brief temptation. He picked up the lamp and led the way around the women's side of the building. This was exactly like the men's quarters except that none of the cots was made up.

"I'll look up the elder in charge," he said. "He'll see that you get bedding. I'm riding south again."

There was surprise and a question in her look, but she said nothing. She unrolled the mattress on the first cot and sat down on it. She looked small and tired and altogether beautiful, Mayberly thought.

He crossed the yard to the meetinghouse and went

inside. The spacious interior had the aspect of a dance hall with the center cleared for activity and chairs lined along the walls. About half the congregation was on its feet, chanting and doing a slow, marching dance. The participants had formed into ranks in two platoons, men in one and women in the other. These faced in opposite directions and were on opposite sides of the room so they could march back and forth past each other. They marched forward in slow cadence to the chant till they reached the end walls, then they marched backward. They chanted the same verse over and over again.

> *I will march, I will go*
> *In this pretty, shining way.*
> *In freedom's lovely valley*
> *On my trumpet I will play.*

Hat in hand, Mayberly stood just inside the doorway and finally spotted Mr. Asbury sitting among the onlookers. Asbury saw him and got up and came toward him. They stepped outside to talk.

Asbury said he would send a woman to the guesthouse to see that Melody was made comfortable. He hadn't heard the explosion, no doubt because of the noise of the meeting.

"You must have a roster of your people," Mayberly said. "Have somebody check. Make sure they are all here. It might be important to be able to swear to that."

"This is a special meeting we called tonight," Asbury said. "We felt the need of sustenance in this time of false accusation and the threat of persecution. If there has been another obfistication—well, the Lord works in mysterious ways."

147

Mayberly asked for a fresh saddle horse and Asbury told him to take his choice of any in the pasture or the barn. Five minutes later Mayberly was on his way.

He followed the wagon road to the river. Then he crossed the bridge and took the river trail, which he judged was more direct and faster for a man on horseback. He had picked a good horse. It held a long-paced, ground-covering trot that was almost as easy on the rider as a single-foot. From time to time, when he was sure of the ground, he urged the animal to lope.

Even so, it was a long, dismal ride. Few stars were out and there was no breeze. There was a clammy warmth to the air that was unusual at this altitude this late at night. It was the kind of night that stirs something poisonous in the nervous make-up of men and animals, something that prods old hunters into carelessness and the hunted into panic. Something that moves medicine men to pinch gunpowder into their faces and shake their rattles.

After a time, he left the river to ride cross-country and along farm roads. He passed the ruins of the guardhouse and came into sight of the phalanstery.

Lanterns bobbed everywhere in an island of hazy yellow-green light and shifting shadows. As he drew closer, he saw half the phalanstery had dissolved to rubble. White-faced people milled, sauntered, darted. Lamps in other buildings flickered. Every window had been shattered.

He swung into the north-south road, skirted the area, and turned at the crossroads. He rode east for a few yards; then he dismounted and left the horse to graze beside the road. He walked toward the crowd in front of the ruined building, thinking of Elwood Snowe and keeping in the shadows. He approached a man standing a little apart from the crowd, a young man in a well-cut suit. He had a shocked, faraway look about him. He didn't take his eyes off the ruined building until Mayberly spoke.

"Anybody hurt?"

"Hurt? Good Lord, sir, the housekeeper and the clerk of the council were killed!"

"What about Dr. Favra?"

"He got a broken arm and I dare say he was thoroughly bruised up. He was lucky, I'd say. He was in the south end of the building."

"What about Elwood Snowe?"

"He's all right. He wasn't in the building."

That just about clinches it, Mayberly thought. Snowe was in this up to his eyebrows. And if he was in it, the Ambrose brothers were in it.

"I've always thought those Shakers a bit on the balmy side," the young man said. "But I always thought them harmless. Who'd dream they were capable of this sort of viciousness?"

"You blame the Shakers?"

"I think everyone does. Oh, it makes sense, I suppose. This was their colony once. I dare say they meant to kill Favra tonight and try to take it back."

"Where can I find Favra?" Mayberly asked.

"He's meeting with some of the councilmen right now. They're at the schoolhouse, I think. He's going to speak to all of us after a bit."

"Thanks," Mayberly said.

He found Captain Hosko and another member of the Patrol at the door of the schoolhouse. Hosko's eyes flicked the big Colt at Mayberly's side.

"First of all, mister, I'll take that gun. Then I have some questions to ask you."

149

Mayberly dug the deputy's badge out of his shirt pocket, held it up for Hosko to see. "That should answer your questions and I'll keep the gun. I want to see Dr. Favra, privately and secretly. Can you arrange it?"

"How do I know that badge is genuine?" Hosko said. "I never saw you in my life until yesterday. Besides, we don't allow outside interference here."

"Captain, one way or another I'm going to see Favra. You can be present. You and no one else. I'll wait in some quiet place and you can bring him to me."

Hosko puckered his lips, tickling his nose with his mustache. "I'll see. I'll speak to Mr. Snowe about it."

"You damn well leave Snowe out of it. You understand that. You go direct to Favra."

"We have our way of doing things, Mr.—Asbury, isn't it?"

"Captain, if you so much as mention this to Snowe, it'll be the biggest mistake of your life. Favra will have your scalp. I guarantee that. I've got a good idea who's behind this bombing. I can't prove it but I can present a pretty good case. Good enough so Favra won't make a mistake of publicly condemning the Shakers tonight. You tell him that, privately, and bring him to me. Right now."

Hosko tickled his nose with his mustache again and then nodded. "I'll see what I can do. You go to the agricultural laboratory and wait."

"Where's that?"

Hosko pointed toward a low dark building not far from the place Mayberly had left his horse. "You wait in the doorway. I'll try to take Dr. Favra to the infirmary to throw folks off the track. I'll bring him out the back door."

Elwood Snowe and five council members sat sideways behind students' desks. Dr. Favra sat behind the teacher's desk. His broken arm had been splinted. He had a flask of brandy on the desk beside him and had been hitting it to ward off shock. A flush was beginning to appear high on his cheekbones, bright in contrast with his white hair and the pallor of his face. He was angry in a stunned, careful way that Elwood Snowe didn't like.

"...Whatever is going on, we're going to get to the bottom of it, and promptly," Favra was saying. "We will add auxiliaries to the Patrol—a hundred men if necessary. We will question every man, woman and child in the colony—beginning with the Shakers. But when I speak to the crowd outside in a few minutes, I am going to call for restraint. In deed and in thought. Moreover, I am going to point out that there is no evidence of an organized conspiracy. This might be the work of one demented person. And when the Shakers are questioned, I want them treated with courtesy and respect. More courtesy and respect than they have been getting recently. I will expect you to instruct the Patrol to this effect, Elwood."

"I certainly will," Elwood Snowe said. "I know I speak for the whole council when I say we respect your levelheadedness, sir. But may I say that a vigorous speech seems to me to be called for tonight? And I think you should mention the *possibility* of a conspiracy. After all, someone tried to kill you tonight. That suggests it. It suggests it strongly."

Favra had a pull at the flask and set it down with a bang. "I'm as mad as you are, Elwood. I'm having all kinds of wild thoughts about what I would like to do to those Shakers. That very anger is a reason for restraint."

Snowe nodded and held his peace. It didn't much matter

if Favra spoke angrily to the people outside or not. They were already thoroughly angry. They would be angrier when the shock had worn off and they had talked things over. He wished Hosko had discovered that trail pointing north that Sip had laid down. He would insist that the Patrol have another look at the roads.

Hosko spoke from the doorway then. "I'm sorry to interrupt, Dr. Favra. May I speak to you in the hall for a moment?"

Favra got to his feet, scowling. He nodded to Hosko.

"We might as well adjourn now, gentlemen. I would like you all to be standing close to me when I speak. It will be a show of unity and determination."

They filed out of the classroom. Favra and Hosko withdrew a little way up the hall and spoke in hushed, earnest tones. Elwood Snowe lingered, pretending to tie his shoe, in hope of overhearing a word or two, but he had no success. He went outside and paused beside the guard at the door.

What happened, Kelly? What's Hosko talking to the doctor about?"

"There's a county deputy here. He wants to speak to Dr. Favra in private."

"A deputy!"

Favra would make short work of him, Snowe thought. He wouldn't want the law sticking its nose in this. Still, it was a bit odd that the man had asked for a private meeting. And that Hosko had gone directly to Favra.

"You have any idea what he wants to talk about?"

"Well—I think you'd better ask Captain Hosko about that, sir."

"Look here, Kelly, I'm asking you."

"The deputy said he had a good notion who blew the

phalanstery. That's all I know."

"Why didn't Hosko come to me like he's supposed to?"

"The deputy asked him not to. He said to keep you out of it."

"He mentioned me by name?"

"Yes, sir."

Snowe produced a snort. He walked away from the schoolhouse and paused at the edge of the crowd milling around the ruins. He found that his hands were shaking and he put them into his pockets. After a moment, Hosko and Favra came out of the schoolhouse. He watched them cross the quadrangle and go into the infirmary. He followed, stopping in the doorway.

The Swiss doctor and two nurses were standing over a white-faced woman who lay on a cot and stared at the ceiling. She was a woman who had been on maid duty at the phalanstery. She was lucky to be alive, Snowe thought. On two other cots, end to end against the wall, lay the sheet-covered bodies of the two persons who had been killed. Snowe asked the doctor how the woman was. The doctor smiled at her and said she was going to be all right. She didn't seem to hear him.

Favra and Hosko were nowhere in evidence and Snowe realized that they must have gone on through the building. He went outside and hurried around to the back. He halted as a match flared in the dark argicultural laboratory a few yards away. Someone lighted a lamp and trimmed it. Snowe changed his position so he could see through one of the paneless windows.

Hosko and Favra were standing with a third man at the far end of the laboratory. The third man was standing with his back toward the window. Snowe moved closer to the

153

window in the hope of overhearing what was being said. There was shattered glass on the gound under the window and it made a loud crunching noise under his feet. Hosko heard it and started across the laboratory toward the window. Snowe darted around a corner of the building.

He ducked into some shrubbery and waited a moment. Then he circled and came back toward the window from a distance. Hosko had gone back across the laboratory and was standing with the other two men. He was facing the window and seemed to be keeping his eye on it. Snowe went as close as he could without running the risk of stepping on glass, but he couldn't hear what was being said.

Dr. Favra raised a hand to his eyes and shook his white-thatched head, apparently in reaction to what the third man was saying. He swayed on his feet, then he moved to a tall laboratory stool and climbed onto it. The third man adjusted his position now. His face was squarely in the lamplight.

Elwood Snowe recognized him at once, but he moved to one side of the window and looked again. And again. There could be no mistake. He retreated into the darkness, stumbling, oblivious to everything but a smothering sense of disaster.

Mayberly! He had trailed the Ambrose brothers here. He probably knew exactly where they were and was making plans to close in on them. He was explaining that to Favra. He was probably asking for the help of the Patrol.

He knows I'm here, too, Snowe thought. The guard at the door said he spoke of me by name. It's all gone sour. If Sip is taken alive, he'll talk. He'll say I planned that express office robbery down at Bramble. He'll say I made a private deal with Fletch to murder the agent. He promised as much in no uncertain terms. He'll talk about the deal we have here too. He'll say I stole the dynamite and made the plans. He'll talk. If he doesn't, Tucker will. Or the girl. Or the boy.

There had been plenty of time for Sip and Tucker to get back to the house by now. Snowe thought of riding over and warning them. But that would be plain foolish. Sip would be suspicious, dangerous, ugly. To go there now would be asking for a bullet in the head.

There was one change. One violent, daring, harum-scarum chance. Just one.

He was running now, pounding over dark ground at the eastern edge of the quadrangle. He reached the stable, found it dark and deserted. He got a saddle on a horse, led it into the open, and mounted.

This was no time to think of what might go wrong, he told himself. It was a time to act. The difference between a great man and an ordinary man was the ability to act swiftly and decisively in time of adversity....

Favra listened. He listened at first with sidelong glances at Hosko that reflected his impatience to get on to more important things than hearing a big hard-faced stranger's speculations. Soon, however, he was listening closely. There was no solid proof yet; the stranger admitted that. But there were too many strange coincidences to be disregarded. The accusations had the feel of truth....

Favra staggered to a stool and got seated on it.

"I find it hard to think straight about anything just now," he said. "What is it you want me to do?"

"First of all, tell your people that there are indications the Shakers aren't responsible for this destruction."

Favra nodded. "I have already decided to tell them not to prejudge anyone. Perhaps I'll put it stronger now."

"I'd bet my last dollar that the man calling himself Johnson is Sip Ambrose," Mayberly said. "But there's a way we can be absolutely certain. I have a woman who can identify him. She's down at the Asbury 'family' for the night. I'll take her to the Johnson place in the morning. When we're sure, I'm going to take the two brothers. Or die trying—which is a possibility. I'll have a better chance of taking 'em alive if I can have the help of the Patrol. I also promised the sheriff he would be in on it. But the reward money is mine, Dr. Favra. That must be understood."

Favra shifted uncomfortably on the stool. It was somehow disappointing to find this man's motives were basically monetary. It was hard to be sympathetic to personal greed. Favra didn't know exactly what the reward for the Ambrose borthers amounted to, but he knew it was a small fortune. The colony could certainly use a share of it.

"I'll not commit myself to that just now." he said. "Things are moving too fast for my stunned brain. Give me time to think."

"Damn it, I'm not sharing that reward." Mayberly said. "I traced the Ambrose brothers here. I'm entitled to it."

"We'll talk later. In the morning."

Favra got down from the stool and walked out of the laboratory into the hallway. Hosko turned down the lamp and he and Mayberly followed.

When they were out of the building, Mayberly lingered near the door while the other two went on around the infirmary. Favra was unsteady and clung to Hosko's arm. When they were out of sight around the building, Mayberly moved to a point where he could see them again. They had come to a stop and were holding a huddled conference. Favra was doing most of the talking. Hosko kept nodding his head.

Mayberly turned toward the place where he had left his horse, suspicion welling in him. It seemed to him that Favra had been giving Hosko instructions. It was possible that he had told him to get some men, go to the Johnson house, and pick up the brothers. Favra didn't seem the sort of man who could be capable of so raw a double cross; yet many people had no scruples about cheating a bounty hunter. And Favra was clearly a law unto himself.

Uncertain of his next move, Mayberly reached the horse and stood brooding in the darkness. He dreaded the long ride back to the Asbury "family," yet he didn't want to spend the night here for fear of being seen by Snowe. Sleeping in the hills would be uncomfortable; he had left his saddlebags and blanket roll back at the Asbury guesthouse.

He turned at the sound of a galloping horse and watched a rider angle away from the buildings and into the road, headed east. Whoever he was, he was in a hurry and he could be going to the Johnson place. Mayberly didn't think it was Hosko, who surely would have sense enough not to approach the Ambrose brothers singlehanded. Snowe? It was possible that Snowe had seen him, Mayberly thought. Hosko had thought he heard someone at the window back at the laboratory. If the rider was Snowe, if he was on his way to warn the brothers, they would slip away before morning. The chase would begin all over again. . . .

The thought was enough to make up Mayberly's mind for him. He got on the horse and rode eastward after the rider.

The sheriff had gone to bed early, but he couldn't sleep. His wife lay on her back beside him, snoring harshly. He dug her in the ribs and she wakened and turned.

The room seemed airless, even though a window was wide open. He got up, worked his feet into carpet slippers, and went to the window. There was no breeze. Here and there a star shone through stringy clouds. Faintly, distantly, a small booming sound rolled through the night. It might have been a single clap of thunder, but he didn't think so. Near as he could tell, the sound came from the direction of the colony. He watched for a long time and saw no lightning flashes in the distance, no sign of thunderheads.

His wife had got on her back again and was breathing raspingly, working up toward full-toned snoring. The sheriff shucked out of his nightshirt and got dressed. He carried his boots into the parlor, lighted a lamp, and pulled them on. He then wrote a note to his wife and propped it up against the lamp.

Twenty minutes later he had roused the livery stable night man, got the county buggy hitched, and was on his way to New Sanity.

15

THE SPECIAL meeting was going to be special indeed. Asbury saw that from the beginning. It was going to be a real old-time all-night roof-rattler.

He was not schooled in the theory of religion, but it seemed to him that Shakerism got pretty well to the heart of the matter. It aimed at a state of consciousness that reached beyond man's usual knowledge of the world. Sometimes this called for oddity in behavior as well as in doctrine—or what misguided folks labeled oddity.

The vague outer nebulae of final truth that man might glimpse could not be approached in terms of the world to be transcended. That, to Asbury, was self-evident. Tonight the brotherhood found itself unable to cope with a worldly threat in a worldly way. So it would lose itself in the Spirit.

The meeting began with the usual kneeling and silent prayer. Shakers considered prayer an individual thing; leaders seldom said words for the whole group. Then the singing started and after a while the marching. This went on for an hour or so, growing in fevor, until finally a sister broke ranks and began to whirl. Another joined her, crying out to the Spirit to descend on her. They whirled until they fell exhausted.

The marching resumed. But Asbury, watched from the sidelines, knew that other breaks in the pattern would take place now, each more strenuous, until a dozen or more Believers were whirling and shaking and spouting revelations all at once.

He saw Mayberly at the door and stepped outside to talk to him. He was sickened to learn that there had been another explosion; but he decided to make no announcement of it, at least not until he had more information. He sent Brother Richard to check the roster, as Mayberly suggested. He also sent a sister to the guesthouse to look after the woman Mayberly had taken there. He then went back and sat down and prayed silently that the new explosion might somehow turn out to be a blessing in disguise. Perhaps it would lead to discovery of the guilty person, he thought, and the Shakers would be exonerated.

After a while the marchers began a new chant and marched backward and forward in quicker rhythm.

> *We love to dance, we love to sing,*
> *We love to taste the living spring,*
> *We love to feel our union grow*
> *While back and forth and back we go.*

Some of those on the sidelines now got up and joined the marchers. Others stood and chanted and marked time. Some of the marchers raised their arms and began to shake.

Across the hall from Asbury, the door opened. A woman stood in the doorway. A dark-faced woman in a poke bonnet. He didn't recognize her. He thought at first that she might be the woman Mayberly had brought to the guesthouse. He hurried across the floor to greet her.

"Welcome!" He had to shout to make himself heard. "Are you Miss Coates?"

He found himself looking into a pair of black eyes squinted against the light. They held a snappish look that flustered him. The woman moved so she could see past him.

"It's a right capersome meeting," Asbury said. "Would you care to sit down and observe?"

The black eyes flicked him again but the woman made no reply. Asbury moved behind her to close the door and saw a small covered wagon standing in the road. She was not Miss Coates, he decided. As he swung the door shut, he got a strong whiff of whisky.

The woman was probably ill, he decided charitably. Lots of folks took a dram for the neuralgia and such. It was not unheard of, either, for an ailing stranger to come to a Shaker meeting looking for a cure. Tales about Shaker cures got spread around among the worldy.

"There's a chair yonder," he said.

Unthinkingly, he violated a Shaker taboo and touched the woman unnecessarily. He touched her elbow. She shook him off with a hard look from the black eyes. Then she raised her hands above her head and leaped out on the floor.

"Hallelooo-o!" she bellowed.

Heads turned. The chanting and marching took on a new vigor.

"Hallelooo-o!"

"Hallelujah!" a woman on the sidelines responded.

The woman in the poke bonnet burst into a song in a squeaky tenor and went into a prancing dance. Asbury had never head the song before and didn't catch the words clearly. Some of those who passed close to the woman gave her strange glances, but others were caught up in her exhilaration.

"Holy Ghost glory!" a young woman shouted.

"Shake off the flesh!" a man cried.

The marching dissolved in discordant frenzy as everybody struck out for himself, dancing, shouting, whirling, shaking. Old Sister Clementine, who was getting on toward eighty, trotted out on the floor and began speaking in tongues. A real old-time meeting, Asbury thought.

"Chain the devil! Chain the devil!"

"A gift! A gift!"

"Shake off the flesh!"

"Shake off the goddamn flesh!" the woman in the poke bonnet bellowed.

Once in his youth, long before he became a Believer, Asbury had attended a sideshow at a county fair. A woman in a grass skirt had danced most shamefully. The gyrations of the woman in the poke bonnet now brought that dance to mind. Asbury chided himself for carnal thoughts and turned his eyes away from her.

She danced close to him and the smell of whisky hit him like a sour wind. He faced up to the truth now. This was no ailing female who had drammed medicinally. The lady was plastered.

She stopped dead still in front of him and studied him a moment. The she put her back to him and crossed the floor in a series of crowhops. Most of the others were too engrossed in individual pursuit of the Spirit to pay much attention to her now.

"Mother Ann!" a woman cried. "Descend, Mother Ann!"

"A gift! A gift!"

"I'm a-gittin' it! I'm a-gittin' the Spirit!"

"Death! Death to our animal natures!"

"Halleloo," the woman in the poke bonnet said. Her

voice was thin now. There was a grayness in her face and she was puffing heavily.

She paused, swaying and looked around in bewilderment. She backed against the wall and for a moment seemed about to collapse. Then she straightened and pulled herself together for a final burst of fervor.

"Halleloo!"

She took a short run and turned a handspring. Actually, it was three-quarters of a handspring. She got herself upside down with good momentum; but then her body hit the floor with a solid slap and she lay still.

This caused little or no lessening of the activity around her. The others gave her a little room and went on with their chanting and shaking and whirling. Two sisters bent over her. Brother Richard was at Asbury's elbow.

"Who is she?"

"I don't know."

One of the sisters came toward them.

"Elder Asbury," she said, carefully keeping alarm out of her voice, "I believe that woman is drunk."

"Let's say she has had an overdose of medication," Asbury said solemnly. "We ought to get her out of here. If we could rig a stretcher...".

"The door has removable hinge pins," Brother Richard said. "We could carry her on that."

Melody Coates was ill at east in the spartan surroundings of the guesthouse. She washed her face, braided her hair, and drank a great deal of cool sweet water the Shaker woman had brought her. She stretched out on her cot without undressing. She fell asleep easily but the noise of the meeting kept waking her.

She wished Mayberly hadn't gone off and left her alone

in this lonely place. She kept hoping he would come back. During the periods of wakefulness, she listened for sound of him on the other side of the partition that ran the length of the building. If she heard him, she would go around and knock on the door, she thought. If she could just see him for a moment, know that he was back, her nervousness would leave her. He would understand that, she thought.

She woke to a sharp knocking on her door and jumped to her feet. She hurried to open it, expecting Mayberly. Instead, she was faced by a Shaker woman with an armful of bedding. Behind her, four men carried a door with an unconscious woman stretched on it.

The Shaker woman was the same who had brought Melody's bedding earlier. Sister Sarah, she called herself. She said tersely that a strange woman had attended the meeting and had been overcome. Melody helped her tuck a sheet around a mattress. Then the four men lifted the woman from the door and brought her inside and put her on the cot. They were ill at ease in the women's quarters and immediately filed out into the night.

Sister Sarah began to remove the woman's shoes. "Truth is, she's intoxicated. On liquor."

"For goodness' sake," Melody said.

"I'll sleep here tonight."

Melody said she would appreciate that. She moved to the head of the cot and untied the ribbon that held a poke bonnet on the woman's head. She lifted off the bonnet. She saw at once that the woman wore a switch. It had been pinned across her head and brought down over her ears. Melody tried to straighten it and it came loose. She laid it aside, thinking that the poor creature had had goodness knew what kind of a hard life. She had cut off her own hair and sold it, likely as not. Or she had had a long illness;

doctors sometimes ordered that a patient's hair be cut off. Then she saw the mangled right ear.

Sister Sarah was tucking a blanket around the woman. Melody grabbed her by the shoulders and backed her away.

"You stay right here," Melody said. "Keep her here if she wakes up. I'll be right back."

"Where are you going?"

"Next door to the men's section. I'll just be a moment."

"The men's section? My dear, we never— What for?"

"Handcuffs," Melody said.

16

ELWOOD SNOWE let the horse slow to a canter and kept it there. He knew what he was going to do and how he was going to do it and he didn't spend much time going over the plan. He thought mostly how it would be afterward with the Ambrose brothers dead and Favra quite possibly dead, too, and Elwood Snowe at the head of the colony. If Favra wasn't killed, he would have to be discredited. That shouldn't be hard to do if the dam failed, the dam that Favra had built.

When Snowe reached the hill where the road bent away to the south, his horse wanted to leave the road and became harder to manage. For some reason, it wanted to follow the wagon track that led up over the hill and down the other side to the Johnson place. Snowe had to fight the animal back onto the road and it gave him trouble all the way to the dam.

There was a zigzag road up the canyon wall that abutted the dam on the west. He rode to the top and saw that the damkeeper's cabin was dark. The dynamite was in a small shed a little distance up the slope behind the cabin. He himself had brought the explosive from Star City and had seen it stored away. He had secretly provided himself with a spare key to the padlock on the shed so he could steal the box he had given to Sip. He had hidden the key under a rock in back of the shed. He found it now without striking a light and went into the shed.

There was a lantern just inside the door. He closed the

door and lighted it, although under ordinary circumstances he would have followed the safer practice of taking the lantern into the open first. There were eleven cases of dynamite, wooden boxes with hinged lids and sealed latches of non-sparking metal. Each contained fifty pounds of dynamite in one hundred and six eight-inch sticks.

Snowe turned the lantern very low and carried six cases into the open, one at a time. While he was doing this, his horse took it into its head to stray down the trail and Snowe had to go after it. He found sash cord, commonly used for bundling charges, and used this to lash the cases onto the saddle. He led the horse down the zigzag road to the foot of the dam.

There was a drainage and inspection gallery with its entrance on the west side of the face of the dam, and he unloaded near it. Then he rode the horse back up to the shed for the other five cases. When he had these lashed to the saddle, he gathered the accessories he would need. A spool of safety fuse and another of detonating fuse. A knife. Sash cord. A box of blasting caps. A cap crimper. He put the fuses and sash cord into a gunny sack and fastened it to the saddle with the boxes of dynamite. Knife, caps, and crimper went into his pockets. He blew the lantern out and carried it as he led the horse back down the embankment.

He tied the horse to a bush near the entrance to the inspection tunnel and unloaded. He lighted the lantern, picked up one of the cases, and stooped into the tunnel. This was an arched gallery five feet high and three wide. It angled upward and inward toward the core of the dam. It was paved with brick and had tile gutters. At intervals of four or five yards, ten-inch pipes projected a few inches from the walls just above the gutters. These, he knew, were perforated on their upper sides to collect seep and run it off.

He reached the end of the tunnel and knew he was within a few feet of the core wall of the dam. He left the dynamite and the lantern and made his way back to the entrance. It was a relief to breathe fresh air and to be able to stand up straight, but he rested only a few seconds. He made eleven trips altogether, carrying the bag of fuses along with the last case of dynamite.

He knew at least a little bit about dynamite. Moreover, he knew the dam. Almost from the day of his arrival at New Sanity, he had taken an interest in its operation and maintenance. This had pleased Favra at first, but recently he had begun to resent it.

Snowe knew of the minor faults in the core wall, indicated by high seepage. Apparently they were not serious in themselves; at least there had been no increase in seepage in the last year and a half. But an explosion of five hundred and fifty pounds of high velocity dynamite near the core would shatter enough of it so that adjacent materials would shift. Moreover, it would subject the whole structure to stresses equal to those of a major earthquake. Surely, the dam would crumble under the pressure of the lake behind it.

He worked rapidly, visualizing the disintegrating face of the dam as it released its solid wall of water on the valley. The hill just downstream would split the flood temporarily. Part of it would sweep up the old overflow channel. It would crush the Johnson house like a toy. Sip and Tucker and Susanna and the boy would scarcely have time to realize what hit them. There was absolutely no chance that they could get to safety. This part of the flood would roar on around the hill in the old channel to rejoin the main rush of water just above New Sanity headquarters.

The buildings there would be flooded, probably washed away. A few of the people might possibly have time to get to high ground, Snowe thought, but they would be the young and agile. Favra would probably be in bed in the infirmary by this time. There was a good chance that he would be drowned. A better than even chance, Snowe thought. ·

He bundled dynamite around a doubled length of detonating fuse until he had a chain of twelve bundles, the contents of one case. He shoved this into one of the drainage pipes to get it as close as possible to the core wall. The pipe was damp, but the paraffin-coated manila wrappers around each dynamite cartridge would keep water from affecting the efficiency of the explosion if detonation was not delayed more than a few minutes.

He had developed a splitting headache. Dynamite did that to you when you worked with it in badly ventilated quarters. He hastily stacked the remaining cases in kind of a staggered pyramid, running the detonating fuse in and out of each. He then punched a hole through a single stick of dynamite and inserted the fuse. He crimped a blasting cap onto the safety fuse and inserted it into the same stick. The detonating fuse would explode instantaneously and set off the rest of the charge. The shot couldn't fail, he assured himself.

He estimated a liberal five yards of safety fuse and cut it off the spool. Safety fuse burned at the rate of two minutes per yard. That would give him ten minutes—more than enough to get out of the gallery and ride around the end of the west abutment to safety. He slit the end of the fuse and touched if off, pressing a match into the exposed powder as the flame flared.

He picked up the lantern, bumping his aching head on

the ceiling as he straightened. He padded down the gallery in mind-numbing pain. Staggering, he bumped into one of the walls and dropped the lantern. It went out and he stumbled on in darkness. The tunnel bent sharply just before it reached the face of the dam. Stooping under the low ceiling, he ran headlong into the wall. He fell hard and lay stunned for a few seconds. He got to his feet and fell again. Something was wrong with his left leg. He must have stepped into the gutter and sprained his ankle, he thought. He staggered to the end of the tunnel and into the warm freedom of the night.

He hopped and hobbled to his horse and untied it. The animal, frightened by his strange movements, wheeled away when he tried to mount. He lost his hold on the reins and the horse bolted. He limped a few excruciating steps after it, calling weakly. It wanted nothing to do with him and trotted off, head high, toward the road and home.

Snowe tried to follow and was overcome with nausea. He sank to his knees and vomited. His head was bleeding, he discovered. A great lethargy seized him. His body seemed an inert mass that wouldn't respond to the commands he gave it. He got to his feet and his ankle stabbed him with screaming pain. A wave of dizziness hit him and he found himself on the ground without any memory of falling. He got to his hands and knees. He told himself there was plenty of time and made himself take a moment's rest. He took several deep breaths and his head cleared a bit. If he could get to the road and a little way up the embankment, he would probably be safe. He began to crawl on his hands and knees, cursing himself for not using more fuse. He was dizzy again but kept on blindly. He didn't even know if he was moving in the right direction and when he realized this, panic took him over completely. He got to his feet, took half a dozen steps, and fell senseless.

17

MAYBERLY KEPT his horse at its easy, road-eating trot, making no special effort to get within sight of the rider ahead. When he reached the foot of the hill west of the Johnson place, he pulled up and listened to the faint sounds of a cantering horse ahead of him to the south. The rider had gone on toward the dam, and Mayberly chided himself for a bad guess.

Still, he swung his horse up the steep trace to the summit of the hill. He looked down on the black oblong of the house with its open door slanting light across the porch to touch a saddled horse in the yard. Now and then a shadow crossed the patch of light as someone inside moved between the door and lamp.

Puzzled by the presence of the horse, Mayberly worked his way along the backbone of the hill to the north, climbing a bit; then he descended the eastern slope to a point behind the house. He tied his horse to some brush near the creek, drew his Winchester from its boot, and moved up the creek on foot. When he was behind the framework of the new barn, he climbed up the slope and around the structure to the pile of lumber in the yard.

There was only the single horse in the yard; the wagon and the other horses had not returned. He crouched in the shadow of the lumber and studied the doorway. He was at an angle here and couldn't see well into the interior. The shadow kept crossing the doorway. It seemed that some-one was pacing back and forth.

A small sound from behind him brought Mayberly around, a single sharp note above the drone of the creek. It could have been the plunk of a small jumping trout or the splash of a dislodged stone. He could see nothing moving in the black line of brush along the creek, but he watched a long two or three minutes before he turned his attention back to the house.

The horse had drifted toward him, stopped to chomp at a tuft of grass. Mayberly straightened and walked past the animal across the yard. He stopped beyond the cast of light where he could see through the open doorway. A woman sat at a table, facing him. Susanna Velasquez. Someone else was at the table on this side, partly hidden by the door jamb. The boy, he decided. A big man moved restlessly around the kitchen. He was dressed like a farmer and was wearing his hat. He was the man Mayberly had seen in the yard, sawing lumber. Sip Ambrose. He was talking, gesturing, plainly upset about something. As Mayberly watched, he picked up a gunbelt and buckled it on over his overalls.

Avoiding the light, Mayberly crossed the yard and stood close to the wall of the house beside the porch. He could hear clearly here.

"If he's drunk, I'll kill him," the man said. "He never did it on a job before. Never till we was done and hid out somewheres. I'll kill him like a dog."

"Sip, we don't know he's drunk," Susanna said.

"He's drunk. What else could it be?"

"He could have been recognized and taken. We have to think of that."

"The wagon wasn't anywhere in that town, I tell you.

Not on the street, not any place around the courthouse, not at the livery.''

"Maybe you ought to go back and try to figure out the tracks again.''

"Near as I could tell from the tracks, he done like he was supposed to. Only he didn't—at least not at the right time. He ain't here. The wagon ain't in town or on the road or no place around the phalanstery. He must've—''

He broke off suddenly. Mayberly dropped to his haunches beside the porch rail. Sip's shadow reached out across the yard as he came to the doorway. He stood there a moment and turned back inside.

"This thing has got me jumpy,'' he muttered.

"He must've what?'' Susanna said.

"He must've took that north road. There's no sense to it a-tall, but it's the only thing I can think of. The son of a bitch got drunk and somehow got by me and took the north road.''

"The Patrol might be heading north, mightn't it, if they blame the Shakers as Mr. Snowe said?''

"I'll go see, I guess. Can't think of anything else.''

Sip was in the doorway again. Mayberly crouched, Winchester ready.

"Go to bed,'' Sip said over his shoulder. "You and the boy. Only don't take your clothes off, boy, you hear? Just your shoes. We could have to move out of here in a hurry.''

"You have only one horse,'' Susanna said.

"If I don't find Tuck by morning, I'll get another someplace.''

"What about me? You going to leave me here?''

"Go to bed.''

Sip strode across the porch and down the steps. As he

turned toward the horse, Mayberly was at his back.

"You're covered. Don't move."

Sip Ambrose halted dead in his tracks. Slowly, he raised his hands to shoulder height. Only then did he turn his head.

Mayberly stepped close and snatched the revolver from Sip's gunbelt. Sip whirled at just the right instant, flinging the muzzle upward so Mayberly's one-handed shot went wild. Sip had the stock of the rifle in his other hand. He sliced it upward in a vicious arc aimed at Mayberly's head.

Mayberly knew the trick and let go the rifle in time to avoid the blow by a whisker. He tossed Sip's revolver to his right hand and cocked it. Sip froze. He dropped the rifle and raised his hands again.

Mayberly moved a few steps backward, circling to put Sip between himself and the doorway. The boy was standing in the doorway. Susanna was not visible behind him. There was no telling what she might do. It was best to shield himself behind Sip as much as possible.

"Step down here, son," Mayberly said. "Your Aunt Melody is not far from here. I'll take you to her."

The boy came to a halt on the steps, staring past Mayberly. Sip, too, was staring. Mayberly took a step sideways and turned cautiously. He found himself looking into the muzzle of a rifle held by Yadkin. Deeds stood a few feet to the right. He, too, held a rifle, aimed at Sip.

"Drop the gun," Yadkin said. "We'll take over, now."

"You can go to hell," Mayberly said. "He's my prisoner."

He put his back squarely to Yadkin. As long as there were witnesses, it seemed a reasonable risk.

174

"Hello, Harry," Sip said to Yadkin.

"Hello, Sip."

"Who are these roosters?"

"This one's a Pinkerton. This here is Mayberly."

"I'm your prisoner, Harry."

"The hell you are," Mayberly said. Then he addressed himself to the boy. "Son, my horse is a piece behind the house, down by the creek. Get him for me."

"We already got him," Yadkin said. "Drop the gun and give up, Mayberly. We got you euchred."

Susanna came into the doorway. She paused a moment and then crossed the porch and put her hands on the boy's shoulders.

"Son," Mayberly said again, "go look for the horses. Bring one for yourself. I'll take you to your aunt."

Yadkin swung the barrel of his rifle against the side of Mayberly's head, bringing dancing lights to his brain and robbing him of co-ordination. The gun slipped from his hand and he staggered toward the porch, fighting to keep his feet. Yadkin's second blow came straight down on his skull and felled him.

He revived to the coolness of a damp cloth on his forehead and found that his head was in Susanna's lap. She was sitting on the porch steps. He sat up, fighting pain that was like a solid thing in his skull. He realized dully that he had been unconscious for some time. Horses were moving in the yard, leather squeaking as men mounted.

They had put the boy on Mayberly's horse. Deeds and Sip were also mounted. Sip's hands were tied in front of him. The reins of his horse were held by Deeds. Deeds had two gunbelts looped over his shoulders. He had a rifle in his saddle boot and another across his saddle. Yadkin was also loaded down with extra weapons and with a white

175

canvas bag tied to his saddle horn. He mounted and waved to the others to move out of the yard.

Mayberly got woozily to his feet. He started toward Sip with the idea of pulling him out of the saddle. Yadkin gigged his horse and bumped him, knocking him flat. By the time Mayberly got to his feet again, the party was moving off. Susanna was beside him.

"Sometimes you lose, Mr. Mayberly."

"They didn't take you," he said stupidly.

"They didn't have a horse for me. Sit down for a moment and rest. Can we make a deal, Mr. Mayberly?"

He picked up his hat, brushed himself off with it, and put it on his throbbing head. He stayed on his feet, fighting shakiness and anger, telling himself to think coldly.

"You don't need a deal," he said. "You're guilty of aiding and abetting wanted criminals, something like that. But your crime is in Montana and they're wanted in Colorado. There's enough legalistic mishmash in that situation so you can feel safe. You might spend a night in jail, but I doubt it."

A little way up the slope, a match flared. The party had stopped. Mayberly squinted into the darkness to try to see what was happening. The match went out.

"Mr. Mayberly, I want to get out of here," Susanna said. "Tonight. I want your help. We can walk to New Sanity headquarters and you can get us horses there. Take me to Spinnerville and hide me till I can get a southbound stage. In return, I'll tell you where Sip and I think Tucker is."

"I know where you think he is. I overheard you talking. And you were only guessing."

Another match flared on the slope. It looked as if the boy was holding it and Deeds or Yadkin got down to shorten the stirrups for him.

"You got a gun around?" Mayberly asked Susanna.

"Yadkin got them all. He went through the house when you were knocked out. He got a bag of hard money that was under Sip's bed too...."

Mayberly started up the slope. She called to him but he ignored her. The match went out. He hoped another would be lighted, but it was not. Dimly, he made out the riders resuming their way up the hill. They were moving fast. He kept after them, feeling steadier.

"Wait!"

Susanna was behind him, running to catch up. He increased his stride but she was quickly beside him. She had picked up a big canteen and was walking with it slung over her shoulder.

"What are you going to do?" she said.

"Get a horse and a gun from Hosko, try to catch 'em before they get to town."

"Please get me a horse too. Hide me and get me on that stage. I'll pay you whatever you ask."

I'm beginning to understand," he said. He reached out and hefted the canteen. "How much you got there?"

She hurried on without answering. He said, "A lot, I guess. It will have to be turned in to the authorities. If it's identifiable loot, it will be returned to its rightful owner."

"I don't really know how much there is," she said after a moment. "It's a wad of bills as big as a brick. Most of them are big bills, I think. I'll pay you a thousand dollars to help me get over the state line."

"Don't be a fool," he said. "Turn the money in before the law has a chance to take it away from you. That will work in your favor. Besides, banks and express companies generally pay a ten per cent reward for the return of loot."

177

"I'd rather have one hundred per cent."

"You're more likely to wind up with nothing but jail."

"You said jail wasn't likely."

"It's plenty likely if you try to slope off with loot."

They were better than halfway up the hill. She had to run every other step or so to keep up with him.

"You ought to take a look at yourself," he said. "You want too much and you want it all at once. There are things more important than money."

She laughed a little wildly. "You say that, Mr. Mayberly? You?"

The night shook then, and the earth under them. They stopped and turned and for one frozen instant they stared toward the dam. They could see little except a vague flat outline between the black shapes of guarding buttes. But disaster was there, too, heard or glimpsed or guessed at.

Mayberly had her by the arm and they were running up the hill with panic in their feet. They reached the top and turned north along the rising chine. He halted, waving her on, and turned to look into the valley to the west.

The riders ahead were one shapeless moving shadow. They had reached the road at the foot of the hill, had turned back when they heard the dam go. They galloped up the hillside now, four abreast, hoof sounds smothered by the roaring night.

He looked southward and saw the unbelievable black avalanche whip into sight, its shining tongue alone wider than the river channel. The first swift, boulder-rolling lash of water might pass below the men and the boy, he thought. But it looked as if the deepening pyramid behind it would catch them.

Susanna called to him. He yelled at her to get higher, get as high as she could. He stayed where he was, helplessly watching the horses strain up the hill. The boy was in the lead now. He was on the horse Mayberly had got from Asbury. A hell of a good horse. He might make it. He might.

Water churned down the valley, trapped between this hill and the ridge across the channel. It quickly rose over the low places in the ridge and poured out across flatter land to the west. Yet it still rose here, too, and swiftly. Three of the riders were caught in it, a racing torrent that boiled around the horses' hoofs and two jumps later was up to their bellies.

The boy was only twenty yards below Mayberly. It looked as if he were out of it; then his horse stumbled to its knees and threw him. Mayberly raced down the slope, passing the horse, which quickly recovered and was safe. The boy was slow to get up. He was caught by the rising water, getting to his feet, falling, getting up again in waist-deep water. Mayberly plunged in and caught his extended hand just as he lost his footing again. Mayberly dragged him to safety, got him to his feet.

"Run, son. Susanna's up there somewhere. Run."

The other horses were only a few yards away, swimming, riders still in saddles. Two were moving with the current. The third, the nearest, swung sideways to it and was rolled under. It reappeared without a rider. Then the man surfaced, raising clenched hands prayer-like above the water. It was Sip Ambrose, Mayberly realized, and his wrists were bound.

Mayberly found himself swimming, or trying to, desperately handicapped by his boots. He bumped into something, a man, fought off the bound, grasping hands and seized him by the hair. He struck out for dry ground with a great clawing stroke and went under. His boots were lead weights that kept pulling him down. He swung with the current, got his head above water. For a miracle, his feet

179

touched bottom and he saw they had been swept to a modification of the hill, a spur that jutted out from the slope. He could not keep his footing but he pushed toward shore, touched again, pushed again. Sip was helping, kicking and pushing. At last they were in waist-deep water and Mayberly could stand, could get Sip to his feet, stagger to shore.

Susanna was there, foolishly pounding Sip on the back in an effort to relieve his sputtering. Sip got his breath and was all right. They scrambled to the crest of the hill.

"That was a brave thing," Susanna said. "A brave, foolish thing."

"Hell," Mayberly said. "He's worth seventy-five hundred dollars."

Sip sank to the ground and lay prone. Mayberly got his breath and went off to look for the boy's horse. He found it standing dejectedly on the small band of road that was left across the hilltop.

The water had topped the ridge to the west and would come no higher up this hill. To the east, where the house had been, there was a swirling black lake. Mayberly could not make out with certainty what had happened to the dam. It seemed to him that only an upper portion of it was gone. If that was true and if the plunging reservoir didn't tear away the lower section, the flood might quickly crest.

He led the horse along the hilltop. He heard a voice ahead in the darkness, a man's voice, vague above the roar of water. He made out moving figures, close at hand but indistinct against the rising backbone of the hill. He left the horse, hurried forward, and almost fell over Susanna, who lay beside a patch of brush. She sat up and blood trickled down her face from a cut on her forehead.

"Sip!" she said. "I untied his hands. He took — my canteen. Then Yadkin came ..."

Mayberly moved toward the figures ahead, slowly now, crouching in the brush. There were two men struggling; then one sank to his knees. The man on his feet was Sip. He raised a revolver above his head and brought it down violently. The kneeling man wrenched away and the blow seemed to strike him on the shoulder. He sank to all fours but did not fall flat. Sip, worn and unsteady, cocked the gun.

"You ready to die, Harry? This is a night of reckonin'. Beg for your life, Harry. You can live maybe two breaths longer if you beg."

A small shape moved up out of the darkness. Sip took a step backward.

"Don't shoot him, Pa. You whipped him. We got to help one another get out of here."

Sip caught the boy by the collar and raised the gun to strike him. Mayberly sprang, caught the lifted wrist, caught the elbow, turned the forearm backward in a arc. The gun flew into the darkness. Sip's arm snapped at the elbow as he went over Mayberly's hip in a backward somersault. Mayberly fell on top of him, putting a knee hard into his gut, throwing punches that took the last fight out of him.

As he got to his feet, the boy handed him the revolver and the canteen. Susanna came up as Mayberly slung the canteen over his shoulder. She laughed wearily.

"I'll hate you someday," she said. "Right now I just want to be alive."

Yadkin had matches in a watertight case and they built a fire. While they were drying out, Deeds wandered dazedly out of the darkness. He was in his stocking feet. He had lost his horse but had managed to shuck his shoes and coat and stay afloat. He had got to shore a considerable distance downstream.

18

IF ELWOOD SNOWE had placed his charge lower in the dam, the whole structure might have given way as he anticipated. Or it might not have. That was a thing for engineers to argue for years to come. As it was, a top third of the center section was cracked and loosened so that it slid and crumbled. Below and at the outer edges, the dam held.

The crushing wall of water, carrying giant fragments of masonry with it, quickly swamped the narrow gulches just below the reservoir. Beyond, the flood reached out over field and pasture, rising swiftly. But this was rolling country and men and livestock were usually able to get to high ground and save themselves.

At New Sanity headquarters the tongue of the flood swept out the bridges and washed away a building that hugged the riverbank; yet its devastation was less than Snowe had visualized. Only part of the eastern arm of the torrent followed the creek course around the hill. The bulk of it crashed on northward in a new channel and came nowhere near the headquarters building.

The people, most of whom were still awake, got to hilltops and rooftops. Many gathered on what was left of the third floor of the blasted phalanstery. Woodpiles and privies were swept away but the buildings stood. Only the injured woman in the infirmary was drowned.

There was little additional attrition of the dam. After the first angry hour, the plunge over the broken wall slackened. By morning it had thinned to something like a normal spill. Waters were already receding in the flooded places. By noon New Sanity headquarters was, in the language of the moment, "dry"—even though the mud was a yard deep. Most of the roads were passable, too, although there was hub-deep water in the low places. Shakers came up from the south with food and blankets and dry clothing for the folks at the headquarters. They brought word of disastrous crop damage in the lower valley. Buildings at the northernmost "family" had been flooded, but the others weren't damaged. There had been no loss of life.

Under Favra's direction, a raft was built and a crew got a line across the swollen river a bit downstream from headquarters. A block and tackle was put to use, a team hitched, and a ferry service established. It was here that Mayberly's party crossed early in the afternoon, leaving their horses behind.

They walked to a camp set up at the crossroads near the phalanstery. The sheriff was here and Mayberly turned Sip Ambrose over to him, along with the canteen Susanna had brought. Yadkin also turned over the bag of coin he had taken from under Sip's bed. It was probably a roll or two of gold eagles short, Mayberly guessed.

He asked for a horse, intending to ride north and look for Tucker. He had just got a saddle on it when the sheriff approached and pointed to a covered wagon lumbering into camp on the rut-sliced north road. It was driven by Mr. Asbury with Melody on the seat beside him. Two saddle horses were tied on behind. Mayberly called the boy and they went to meet it.

Melody climbed down from the seat and Stevie rushed into her arms. There were squeals and smiles and kisses. She was clearly close to tears but she held them back. Stevie, after his first joyous outburst, seemed embarrassed by it all. Melody faced Mayberly and the small crowd that had gathered.

"I've got Tucker Ambrose in the back," she announced.

Mayberly sloshed through the mud to the tail of the wagon and had a look. Tucker Ambrose in woman's clothes, hands cuffed behind him, lay curled in the wagon bed with his head on Mayberly's blanket roll. He was soundly asleep.

"She done it," Asbury said. "All by herself. She recognized him and put the shackles on him teetotaciously by herself."

Yadkin, who was standing beside Deeds, burst into high-pitched laughter.

"You've got to share it after all, Mayberly! The little lady is entitled to the bounty on Tucker. And you brought her here! You outsmarted yourself, I'd say."

Mayberly turned away toward the head of the wagon. Melody hurried after him and caught his arm.

"You're entitled to part of it—most of it," she said. "You traced them here...."

He shook her off rudely and stalked across the camp to the horse he had borrowed. He uncinched the saddle and threw it angrily to the soggy ground. He slipped off the bridle and turned the animal loose with a slap on the rump. Susanna was standing with some women a little distance away and she came toward him.

"They've got Tucker?"

Mayberly scowled at her. "They have."

184

"Do I have to be taken in too?"

"I don't see much sense in it."

"Then I'll stay here. I think I'll settle here. Dr. Favra says I can stay as long as I like."

Back at the wagon, Melody stood with her arm across Stevie's shoulders and watched Mayberly.

"He's impossible," she said. "He's just simply the surliest, worst-tempered, most impossible man I've ever met!"

Deeds was watching her closely. He laughed and said, "I wish you'd say that about me in that tone of voice."

"He saved my life," Stevie said. "He came into the water after me."

"He did?" She was too absorbed in her own feelings to be much impressed.

"I don't think he's so bad-tempered either."

"He hates me," Melody said. "I happend to find Tucker drunk and I put Mayberly's handcuffs on him and now he hates me."

The sheriff and Dr. Favra had come up and were standing beside Deeds.

"All he's lived for is that bounty money. He's lived for it for four years;" the sheriff said. "Ma'am, a few days ago I had a letter from H. B. Tovey of the Bell and Tovey Express Company. Maybe I know something about Mr. Mayberly that you don't. . . .

"Four years ago he had a little two-coach stage and express line. He owned it. It ran from the Lucky Cut diggings to a town named Bramble. The Lucky Cut strike was new then. The big companies hadn't moved in and the whole gulch was a string of one-man placer claims. Some of the glory-holders hit it pretty big. They shipped their gold dust out by way of Mayberly's stagecoach. He would hold the dust at his Bramble office for the Bell and Tovey coach, which came through every other day or so. Bell and Tovey would take the gold on to their bank in Durango.

"Well, the Ambrose boys hit Mayberly's office when he had around twenty-five thousand dollars in gold in his safe. They killed his agent and got the gold.

"It isn't customary for a small stage line like that to guarantee shipment for the simple reason that a sizable loss would put the company into bankruptcy and the shippers would lose out anyway. So Mayberly was under no legal obligation to reimburse those miners. But he scraped together everything he had in the world, sold his company to Bell and Tovey, and raised enough to pay back almost half the losses. He gave the miners notes for the rest—at interest. Then he set out after the Ambrose brothers to collect the reward and pay off the notes. I guess he didn't figure on spending four years at it, but he did. With the interest and the money he's spent on the hunt and all, the reward just about covers what he owes. You see why he was so set on collecting it."

She was still watching Mayberly, who had turned away from Susanna and was crossing the camp to where Sip Ambrose sat on a log between Hosko and another member of the Patrol. There were tears in her eyes now.

"Yes," she said faintly. "I see."

"There's a bit more to the story," Dr. Favra put in. "Mr. Mayberly told it to me last night. A man named Elwood Snowe worked in Mayberly's office as assistant to the agent. After the agent was killed in the robbery, Snowe got his job. He continued in it for a few months after Bell and Tovey bought the company. He also took up with the agent's widow. Nobody suspected him of being involved in the robbery until she accused him. He helped plan it, she said, and he let the Ambrose brothers know when there was a sizable amount of gold in the safe. She didn't have solid evidence, but she made a convincing enough case against Snowe so that Tovey fired him. Snowe tried to kill her before he left town—or somebody did. Blew up her house with dynamite.

"Snowe came up here and joined the colony. He was the kind of hard-working fuss-budget we needed and he did well. I suspected he was ambitious, but I didn't realize he was mad. The damkeeper brought in his body a little while ago. There was a box of blasting caps and a cap crimper in his pockets."

Mayberly and Hosko came up to the wagon with Sip Ambrose between them. Sip was pale and shaken from the pain of his broken arm. For a moment he and Dr. Favra confronted each other, each with an arm in a sling. No words were spoken. Sip then faced Melody. He stared at her a moment and said, "You here?" and let himself be led on around the wagon.

Melody caught Mayberry by the arm. "Please listen. I don't want reward money paid for Stevie's uncle. I won't accept it. You can have it all."

"Don't be a fool," Mayberly said.

He laid a big hand on each of her shoulders and moved her aside. As he did so, he met her eyes and was surprised by the intensity with which they were fixed on him.

"Take the money," he said more gently. "You've got a boy to raise."

He went to the back of the wagon and climbed in after Sip. The sheriff handed him a key to the handcuffs that pinned Tucker's arms behind him. Mayberly freed one of Tucker's hands and cuffed the other to Sip's good arm. Tucker woke, took a wild-eyed look around him, and groaned. Sip cursed softly. Mayberly climbed through the opening at the head of the wagon and onto the seat.

Her eyes were green, he thought. Really hazel, he supposed, but they had seemed green a moment ago when she looked at him. It was strange how intent they were, how eager for his approval. Damn it, he would remember that look as long as he lived.

The sheriff was with her now, taking her and the boy toward his buggy. Mayberly swore aloud. He dropped off the wagon and began barking orders.

"Harry, you take one of those saddle horses and follow the wagon in. There's a saddle over there in the mud. Deeds, you drive the wagon." He beckoned to the boy. "Son, would you like to ride the other horse?"

"Sure," Stevie said.

"Captain Hosko will find you a saddle. Sheriff, why don't you ride the wagon with Deeds, keep an eye on the prisoners?"

The sheriff was a solemn man and not used to taking orders, but he chuckled softly.

"Welcome back to the human race," he muttered. Only Melody heard him.

"What do you mean by that?"

"I think you're about to find out."

He moved off toward the wagon, passing Mayberly on the way.

"Where do I ride?" Melody said as Mayberly came up.

He took her by the arm, helped her into the buggy, and climbed beside her.

Dr. Favra, Captain Hosko, and Mr. Asbury watched them turn into the road and move off toward Spinnerville— the wagon, the two riders, the buggy. Mr. Asbury took a long look at the couple in the buggy and supposed he should be ashamed of himself. There was a Shaker regulation against watching the carnal caresses of worldly folk. He guessed he would have to confess in meeting.